Look for other
Wing Commander books by
HarperEntertainment

WING COMMANDER

Junior Novelization by Peter Telep
From the screenplay by
Kevin Droney and Mike Finch

Based on the characters
created by Chris Roberts

HarperEntertainment
A Division of HarperCollins*Publishers*

HarperEntertainment

A Division of HarperCollins*Publishers*
10 East 53rd Street, New York, NY 10022-5299

This is a work of fiction. The characters, incidents, and dialogues
are products of the author's imagination, or if real, are used ficti-
tiously. Any resemblance to actual events or persons, living or
dead, is entirely coincidental.

First printing: March 1999

Printed in the United States of America

ISBN 0–06–106556–0

Visit HarperEntertainment on the World Wide Web at
http://www.harpercollins.com

10 9 8 7 6 5 4 3 2 1

P
R
O
L
O
G
U
E

VEGA SECTOR FLEET
HEADQUARTERS

TERRAN
CONFEDERATION
ASTEROID WORLD
PEGASUS

MARCH 15, 2654
0900 HOURS
ZULU TIME

ULYSSES CORRIDOR

700 LIGHT YEARS
FROM EARTH

Nineteen-year-old Radar Officer Thomas Sherryl sat at his console in Pegasus Station's NAVCOM control room. He stared through a wide viewport at the swirling blues and reds of the Charybdis Quasar. He looked past the whirlpool of gasses, past the black hole lying at the quasar's core like a giant mouth, until he imagined a glowing blue planet called Earth.

Thomas Sherryl dreamed of things green. Of the smell and taste of real air. Of foamy ocean waters rushing up and across his chest. Of beach barbecues. Of friends. He no longer sat in his chair, surrounded by billions of tons of durasteel and ice-slick rock; he no longer felt the rumble of the naval base's enormous Ion engines moving the asteroid deeper into the corridor; he no longer had to work the night shift and look after instruments that did a fine job without his help. Thomas Sherryl had found his freedom. *Good-bye towers, gun emplacements, and antennae. Good-bye Confederation capital ships sitting in your spacedocks. I'm no longer stuck on this rock. I got a ticket out. And it's a ticket no one can take away.*

"Hey, Tom? Can you cover for me?"

Robbed of his fantasy, Thomas Sherryl scowled at fellow Radar

Officer Rick Adunda as the other man set down his half-full coffee mug and left before Thomas replied.

With a loud sigh that drew stares from the other people on duty, Thomas switched seats to Rick's console and studied the long-range sensor report: a blank screen. He eyed his own short-range display and found the same.

Then he looked to Rick's coffee mug as it began to vibrate.

A shadow passed over the viewport, followed by a second, then a third.

Muffled explosions sounded from outside the control room.

Jakoby, the stocky security officer on duty, rushed to the viewport. "Kilrathi fighters," he said stiffly.

Alarms blared. Overhead lighting switched to the dim red of battle. Behind Thomas a panel of life-support monitors sizzled and shorted out. He glanced to a bank of screens that showed images from the station's outside cameras:

Twelve comm dishes on the base's northwest side blew apart under the continuous Particle cannon and Meson fire.

Dozens of Dralthi medium fighters swooped down and caught the great Confederation cruisers and destroyers still sitting helplessly in their berths. The fighters resembled glistening gray discs cut through their centers by sleek, single-point cockpits. Heat-seeking missiles streaked away from them, locking onto the Confed ships' now-warming engines. The cruisers and destroyers retaliated with streams of tachyon fire, but dozens of missiles navigated through the laser bolts to impact on and weaken the Confed ships' shields. Another wave of those missiles would tear the ships apart.

A drumming sound seized the NAVCOM control room as asteroid-based gun batteries finally came on line, shooting thick bolts of anti-starcraft fire.

Thomas kept a white-knuckled grip on his chair as he continued to watch, growing more afraid. Like an angry swarm of plastisteel insects, the fighters dove at the station, dropped their bombs, and pulled up, leaving trails of floating debris in their wakes. For every Dralthi destroyed, another soared through the rubble.

One of the heavy cruisers, the *Iowa*, launched a half-dozen F44-A

Rapier medium attack fighters. The Rapiers had short, silver wings and brass-colored noses shaped like barrels that rotated as they fired lasers. The Rapiers were a very powerful fighter. But as they cleared the flight deck, Kilrathi fighters destroyed them with Meson and missile fire that fully covered each ship before blasting it to gleaming fragments.

Something struck heavily on Thomas's shoulder. He turned to find Rick Adunda staring wide-eyed at him. "What are you doing?"

"I, uh, I don't know. I guess, well—"

"Make your report!"

Thomas swallowed and looked at his scope. "I count one-nine-zero bogies inbound. Vector three-seven-four, attack formation."

"Shields are not *responding*," Security Officer Jakoby announced.

The viewport filled with a harsh white light that peeled off the blackness of space. A tremendous thunderclap shook through the entire station as though a fusion bomb had detonated at its core.

"I don't believe it," Ordnance Officer Scott Osborne said, squinting at the viewport as the glare faded. "That was the *Iowa*." He turned toward Thomas, his face growing pale.

"Confirmed," Communications Officer Rene Gemma said. "The *Iowa* is gone. And the *Kobi*."

Admiral Bill Wilson double-timed into the control room with an armored Confederation Marine in tow. He wiped the sweat from his bald head, and his face seemed to grow thinner as he stared out the viewport with weary eyes. He turned to Thomas. "Status?"

Thomas jerked and studied his screen. "Four Kilrathi capital ships coming to bear, Admiral. They are powering weapons."

With a crooked grin, Wilson asked, "How did they get past our patrols?"

"We lost contact with our patrols for a few minutes," Comm Officer Gemma said. "But we reestablished. I thought it was quasar interference. The enemy must've taken them out and transmitted false signals."

Security Officer Jakoby ran to his terminal. He touched the

screen several times. "We have a station breach. Levels seven, eleven, and thirteen. Kilrathi Marines."

Wilson hurried to a bank of security monitors beside Jakoby. Thomas stood to peer over the admiral's shoulder.

Towering forms in copper-colored armor walked through the dim corridors, throwing weird shadows on the walls. Rebreather tubes partially hid their faces and snaked down from long heads to bulging chests. Green fumes trailed behind them as they pounded forward.

A pair of Confed security officers fired at the aliens. Two of the Kilrathi withstood the point-blank hits and thundered on to grab the officers. Thomas turned away as he listened to the women shriek, gurgle, and fall silent.

"They're headed for Command and Control," Jakoby reported.

Thomas may have only been a radar officer, but he knew very well what the aliens wanted. He flicked his gaze to the opposite end of the control room, to the massive computer system shielded by a synthoglass wall, a mainframe that represented the very heart and brain of Pegasus Station. At the system's center lay that small, most precious black box with the letters "NAVCOM" written across its side.

Clenching his teeth, Wilson charged toward the computer system. "Destroy the NAVCOM AI. Now!" he ordered Benjamin Ferrago, the chief navigator.

Ferrago typed frantically on his touchpad, then, balling his hand into a fist, he smashed a glass panel to gain access to a red handle. He threw the handle forward and looked to the black box. Nothing happened. "Command codes have been overwritten."

Wilson whirled and took the Confed Marine's conventional rifle, dropped the slide back, then aimed at the NAVCOM. Thomas flinched as uranium-depleted rounds ricocheted off the synthoglass. Wilson emptied the entire clip before turning the rifle around. With a howl, he charged toward the NAVCOM and drove the rifle's butt into the glass. The stock shattered.

Another concussion echoed from outside. The lift's massive, reinforced doors began distorting, bending in, as the Kilrathi Marines outside fired at it.

"Here," Rick said, slapping a sidearm in Thomas's hand. He winked. "Special *arakh* rounds. Kilrathi catnip. We Terrans stick together."

"Where'd you get this? We're going to get in—"

"Big trouble? You kidding me?" Rick clicked off the safety of his own pistol. "Let's go."

Thomas followed Rick past the radar and navigation stations to a partition opposite the lift doors, where they huddled and watched the doors grow hotter and weaker.

Admiral Wilson regarded Comm Officer Gemma with a serious look. "Prepare a drone. Get me a coded channel."

Gemma seemed lost for a moment, then she touched the correct keys and nodded to the admiral.

Wilson faced the camera at Gemma's station as it turned toward him. "This is Admiral Bill Wilson, Pegasus Station commanding officer. Four Kilrathi capital ships are closing. Station has been breached. They want the NAVCOM."

The lift doors blew off their glide tracks and *thwacked* the deck with twin thuds. A cloud of toxic smoke swelled into the control room. Within that smoke, Thomas saw the outline of a Kilrathi Marine as it bent down and ignited its weapon.

Rick pumped rounds into the smoke, as did some of the other officers. Thomas saw a half-dozen more outlines appear behind the first, and the sight sent him ducking behind the partition.

"Drone away!" Gemma shouted.

Thomas looked back at the viewport. The tiny drone streaked away from the dying station, bound for the nearest Confederation carrier, the *Concordia*, some twelve hours away. It passed in front of the Kilrathi battle group that included a dreadnought, two destroyers, and the largest vessel, a Snakeir-class cruiser. Transports and smaller escort ships flew next to the capital ships for protection.

An explosion stung Thomas's ears, and he saw Rick fall against the partition. Rick had been shot in the chest.

Thomas wanted to act, but he could only tremble. He heard heavy footsteps. Close. Loud breathing, mechanized. *Oh, God. What's that smell?* He looked over his shoulder at the Kilrathi

Marine standing over him, its polished armor reflecting explosions from outside, its pale yellow eyes growing wide.

As Thomas lifted his pistol, the Kilrathi plucked it from him, grunted, and kicked him onto his back. The soldier pressed its boot on his chest, cutting off his air.

In those last seconds, Thomas took himself away from Pegasus, through the jump point at Charybdis, and back home to his friends, to his family, to all that he loved.

CONCORDIA
BATTLE GROUP

MARCH 15, 2654
2100 HOURS
ZULU TIME

42 HOURS
FROM EARTH

In classic battle group formation, the Confederation-class carrier *Concordia*, flagship of the 14th Fleet, glided majestically through space, along with five cruisers, five destroyers, and ten support ships.

Admiral Geoffrey Tolwyn stepped across the carrier's wide bridge to lock gazes with Commodore Richard Bellegarde, who had just exited the lift.

"Did we get it, Commodore?" Tolwyn asked.

Bellegarde nodded. "It's just been decoded." He hurried toward a video monitor at the commander's station. Tolwyn fell in behind him.

The screen lighted with a shaky image of Admiral Bill Wilson, whose eyes pleaded as he spoke. "The NAVCOM command codes were somehow overwritten. We can't shut it down, can't destroy it. Station self-destruct programs have been locked, passwords changed. I'm sorry, Geoff. I'm so sorry." Laser fire pierced the air around Wilson. Small explosions lit the shadowy command and control room behind him. Then static whisked away his face.

Commodore Bellegarde paced the bridge. "I've been considering ways Wilson could've protected it from them. But that doesn't matter. If they have the Pegasus NAVCOM—"

"Calm down, Richard. Let's assume they have it," Tolwyn said. "Suggestions?"

"Let's go after them."

"Exactly. And I'm sure the Kilrathi counted on that." Tolwyn turned toward the open area between the commander's station and the lift. "Tactical. Give me the Vega and Sol sectors."

A swirling holographic projection took shape as overhead lights dimmed. Dozens of star systems appeared in each of the selected sectors, their tiny planets rotating in real time about their suns. Glowing blue orbs showed the positions of Confederation capital ships. Red orbs representing Kilrathi cruisers, dreadnoughts, and destroyers dotted the display like blood. The Pegasus Station's last known location stood as a small blue dot at the center of the picture. Behind it, thin white lines formed a tube labeled the Ulysses Corridor. The tube stretched toward a small model of the Charybdis Quasar. Hundreds of yellow lines stemmed from the quasar's back, each representing a path through space-time. One yellow line, much thicker than the others, led directly to the Sol system, to Earth.

Tolwyn walked into the projection, concentrating on the images. As he neared the Sol system, the holograph zoomed in on Earth, illustrating the precious planet in sharp detail. A hurricane swirled off Florida's east coast. Clouds blanketed California. Lightning backlit the thunderheads. Tolwyn glanced at Bellegarde. "What is the fleet's position?"

The commodore stepped closer to the holograph and gestured toward the blue dots. "We're spread all over the sector." He rushed to the commander's station and tapped in coordinates on a touchpad. Then he looked up and shook his head. "The earliest our advance elements could reach Sol is forty-two hours. And that's piecemeal and taking risks with the jumps, sir. If we do make it within that time frame, we'll be breaking every Confederation jump record."

"And with the NAVCOM, the Kilrathi can reach Earth in under forty hours through the Charybdis Quasar." The irony tasted so bitter in Tolwyn's mouth that it made him cringe. "A mere two hours could decide the outcome of this war." He looked away, glaring into nothingness. "Signal all ships to mark our course and make full speed for Earth."

"All ships to mark course and make full speed for Earth. Aye-aye, sir," the commodore said. He spun on his heel toward the situational display on his monitor.

Tolwyn stared at the holograph once more, his gaze directed to the Vega sector and traveling past McAuliffe to Trimble to Baird's Star. "Now. I need to know what the Kilrathi are up to. I need eyes and ears, and I need intelligence. Do we have any ships left in Vega?"

"We have seven capital ships in that sector, sir," Bellegarde answered. "The closest one to the Pegasus Station's last known coordinates is the *Tiger Claw*. But she's in the Enyo system and out of communication range. A drone will take two standard days to reach her."

Tolwyn moved toward a blue orb that quickly formed into an image of the Bengal-class carrier *Tiger Claw*, 700 meters of Confederation fury. Then he accidentally spotted a tiny dot on the projection. Granted, whatever ship it represented lay in the Sol sector, but judging distances and factoring in a jump point, it might be within communication's range and might be able to reach the *Tiger Claw* in time. He pointed at the dot. "Who's this?"

Bellegarde studied the holograph, then typed on his pad. "It's a requisitioned merchantman, sir. The *Diligent*."

"The *Diligent*?" Tolwyn watched as the dot grew into the shape of an old transport vessel.

"She's captained by James Taggart," Bellegarde added.

"Can you pull up her log?"

"Already have. She's en route to the *Tiger Claw* with two replacement pilots: First Lieutenants Todd Marshall and Christopher Blair."

"Open a secure channel to the *Diligent* immediately. I need to speak to her captain—"

"Right away, sir."

"—and this First Lieutenant Blair."

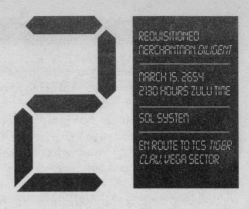

REQUISITIONED
MERCHANTMAN DILIGENT

MARCH 15, 2654
2130 HOURS ZULU TIME

SOL SYSTEM

EN ROUTE TO TCS TIGER
CLAW, VEGA SECTOR

First Lieutenant Christopher Blair lay sprawled out and bare-chested on his rickety bunk in one of the *Diligent*'s tiny cabins. Trying to ignore the uncomfortable surroundings, Blair read his hard copy of *Claw Marks*, the onboard magazine of the TCS *Tiger Claw*, a gift from one of his flight instructors. He absently touched the four-inch-long silver cross hanging around his neck. From a distance, the object appeared like a cross set against a rising sun.

Out of the corner of his eye, Blair saw a bright flash appear on the shelf above his head. Merlin had decided to show himself. The small, holographic old man was created by Blair's Portable Personal Computer. The computer was a tiny device in Blair's wrist, and Blair could use the computer by speaking with Merlin. The little man tossed his waist-length ponytail over his shoulder, then smoothed out his black tunic and breeches, as though he had been somewhere to wrinkle them. "I know there's a war going on—but a requisitioned merchantman? What are we on, a garbage run? Delivering groceries?" Merlin's clean-shaven face tightened like a piece of stretched leather.

Blair ignored him, having learned since age five that Merlin's complaining would soon stop if he didn't have an audience.

"The *Diligent*?" Merlin continued. "Please—the *Dilapidated* is more like it. The *Deluded*. The *Dilatory*."

Frowning, Blair glanced at the upset little man. "*Dilatory*?"

Merlin snorted. "Of course. Inclined to delay, tardy, slow." He smirked. "I'm not keeping you up, am I?"

"Where did you pick up that sarcasm? My father didn't put that in your program. And I know I didn't."

"I downloaded it from the mainframe at the academy while you were in—" Merlin looked up.

"What is it?"

"Lieutenant Marshall is approaching the hatch."

Slapping the magazine over his chest to conceal his cross, Blair flinched a little as the hatch cycle opened and Todd Marshall stepped into the cabin, his regulation blue uniform hanging loosely from his skinny frame, his short blond hair brushing along a sweaty pipe. He raked fingers through his hair, looked angrily at the conduit, and muttered, "What a bucket." Then that slightly crazed gleam returned to his eyes, and his oversized Adam's apple worked overtime. "Up and at 'em. Captain wants you on the bridge. Top priority."

"Really? For what?"

Marshall shrugged, moving around the bunk to stare at Merlin. "He didn't sound thrilled. Come on. We'd better get upstairs." Marshall started for the door.

"I'll meet you," Blair said, reluctant to rise and reveal his cross.

Marshall began to mouth something, then simply shrugged and left.

Blair sat up and took in a long breath. A chill ran up his spine as he whispered the words, "Top priority." He reached for his shirt and hurried from the bunk.

As Blair entered the *Diligent*'s bridge, he got the feeling that he was inside the stomach of a robot who really liked spicy food. Tubes and wires were everywhere. He found Marshall seated to starboard in the co-pilot's chair, studying a navigation screen mounted on a swivel arm. He saw the captain stepping out from the galley next to the bridge, blowing on a steaming mug of coffee.

Captain James Taggart hadn't said much during the voyage. His silence, Blair figured, came from the embarrassment of commanding a tape-and-coat-hanger transport like the *Diligent*. Funny, though. Taggart didn't look the part of gypsy cabby contracted by the military. Dark, neatly groomed hair. A face that barely showed his middle years. And there seemed something rugged, something handsome, something pirate-like about the guy that made you just know he had seen a lot more in the universe than would ever escape his lips. Marshall could take a few lessons from the man.

Blair found the captain's gaze. "Sir?"

But the man's stare lowered to Blair's chest, and a strange look came over his face.

A quick glance down revealed that Blair's cross had slipped out from behind his V-neck shirt. He quickly tucked it behind the fabric and stiffened nervously to attention, waiting for a severe interrogation.

"I don't know who you know, Lieutenant, but you just received a Confed One Secure Communication." Taggart gestured with his coffee mug toward the bridge's center console.

Blair sighed with relief over the captain's decision to ignore the cross, then went to the console, slid over to the comm screen, and keyed an activation code on the touchpad.

The screen filled with the God-like face of a man for whom the phrase "living legend" fit very well. "Admiral Tolwyn."

"At ease, Lieutenant."

"Yes, sir."

"I need a favor," Tolwyn said matter-of-factly, his gray eyes flashing.

Blair swallowed. "Anything, sir."

"You're currently outbound for Vega sector and the *Tiger Claw*. I need you to hand-deliver an encrypted communications disc to Captain Sansky. Message is incoming."

As he waited for the download to complete, Blair grew more confused. The comm recorder beeped. He removed the minidisc and held it up. "Begging the Admiral's pardon, sir, but why not send it on a drone to Pegasus? It would be quicker—"

Slowly, Tolwyn shook his head, driving Blair into sudden

silence. "The Pegasus is gone, destroyed by a Kilrathi battle group twelve and a half hours ago."

Blair's mouth fell open.

"See that Captain Sansky gets that disc," Tolwyn added.

"With all due respect, sir, why me?"

Tolwyn's lips curled in a smile. "Right now you're all I've got." His gaze dropped a moment as he seemed to consider something. "I fought with your father in the Pilgrim Wars. He was a good man—you look like him."

"People say I have my mother's looks, sir."

At the mention of Blair's mother, the admiral's eyes narrowed, as though he remembered something. "Yes, it must've been hard. They were both good people. Godspeed. Tolwyn out."

On the *Concordia*'s bridge, Admiral Geoffrey Tolwyn read the obvious look of displeasure on Commodore Bellegarde's boyish face. The commodore rarely wore that look, and Tolwyn found it impossible to ignore. He cocked a brow. "You don't approve, Richard?"

"Of using Blair's kid? No, sir. I do not."

"Why?"

Bellegarde stepped forward. "I think we both know why."

The *Diligent*'s navigation screens woke from their powerless sleep to create 3-D grids as Captain James Taggart began tapping in coordinates. Blair stood behind him, watching. "This milk run just got a little more interesting," the captain said. "Set a course for Beacon One-four-seven, one-quarter impulse."

Marshall nodded and worked his touchpad. "Course for One-four-seven. One-quarter impulse." He frowned at a flashing red warning that appeared at the top of his screen. "One-four-seven is off-limits, sir. There's a one-hundred-thousand-kilometer no-fly zone around it."

Taggart puffed air. "I said *Beacon* One-four-seven. It's a short-cut. Lose the sir."

With an exaggerated shrug, Marshall regarded his screen, banged in the course, then booted the engage pedal.

As Taggart fell back into his chair and yawned, Blair noticed a small, dark tattoo on the man's neck. Blair recognized the writing: a set of four vertical lines that made up the Kilrathi language. Taggart caught him staring, and Blair looked away.

The *Diligent* streaked by the planet Pluto, on its way toward Beacon 147 near the edge of the solar system.

Taggart got abruptly to his feet. "I'll be in my quarters. Call me when we come within a hundred klicks of the beacon."

"You got it," Marshall said. He waited for the captain to leave, then whispered to Blair, "I don't trust this guy."

3

KILRATHI BATTLE
GROUP

SNAKEIR-CLASS
CRUISER KIS
GRIST'AR'ROC

MARCH 16, 2654
2140 HOURS ZULU TIME

ULYSSES CORRIDOR,
VEGA SECTOR

39 HOURS 20 MINUTES
FROM CHARYBDIS
QUASAR JUMP POINT

For the fourth time, Captain Thiraka nar Kiranka walked through the dense green air that filled the *Grist'Ar'roc*'s bridge to check the radar screen. The attack on Pegasus Station had gone exactly as planned. The absence of difficulties had Thiraka wondering when those difficulties would arrive. His experience fighting humans told him they always did.

Thiraka was born of the most powerful clan on Kilrah, but his father did not believe him worthy of the clan. His father did not believe he could present even a single human death as a gift to Sivar, war god of the Kilrathi people. And his father's beliefs were known by everyone. Thiraka guessed that most of his crew doubted his capabilities. The presence of Kalralahr Bokoth, the Kilrathi fleet's most famous admiral, made Thiraka feel weak and helpless. The admiral had taken over Thiraka's ship and his battle group. *I am a lowborn peasant at the kalralahr's beck and call,* he thought. *I am supposed to be a kal shintahr, a captain.*

Commander Ke'Soick rested a heavy paw on Thiraka's shoulder. "Our officers complain that you're oversupervising them. I've watched you check this screen four times now. Should the third fang here find a discrepancy, he'll report it directly to you."

Thiraka lowered his massive brow. "To me and not the kalralahr?"

"We've only served a short time together, but I already know your pain. You can rely on my loyalty, Kal Shintahr. I'm oathsworn to you and you alone."

Pursing his lips, Thiraka nodded. "A debt is owed. A debt shall be repaid."

"Have you forgotten how your family strengthened my clan by killing the weakest of us? Now we rise in power and serve aboard the empire's deadliest cruisers and dreadnoughts. But my clan also believes that those who bargain with the humans are the lowest of born, cowards despised and condemned by Sivar."

Thiraka moved closer to his commander, and with eyes capable of seeing the infrared spectrum, he looked to see if others watched. "Those opinions are better kept silent. But, dear Ke'Soick, I agree."

Behind them, the lift doors parted to reveal Kalralahr Bokoth. Without a word, the admiral paraded across the bridge, his armor flexing, the colorful clan and battle plumes tied at his shoulders fluttering behind him. He paused at the forward viewport to gaze at the quasar.

"And thoughts become flesh," Ke'Soick said, eyeing the kalralahr with hatred.

Second Fang Norsh'kal, tactical officer, approached them with a computer slate. "Kal Shintahr. Sector report of Confederation ship movements." He offered the slate.

But Thiraka had grown tired of staring at holos and computer screens. "Read them to me."

The Second Fang purred his acknowledgment. "One vessel remains in the sector, the TCS *Tiger Claw*. Intelligence reports that she is still out of communication range with her fleet and holding position."

"Very well," Thiraka said. "Your report tells me nothing new."

"But Kal Shintahr. One of our surveillance stations on the border of Sol sector intercepted and decoded part of a long-range communication from the *Concordia* to a merchantman bound for the *Tiger Claw*. An officer on board that merchantman is delivering an encoded message to the carrier's captain."

"When will the merchantman reach the *Tiger Claw*?"

"We're not sure, Kal Shintahr. The merchantman is headed toward Beacon One-forty-seven, just outside the Sol system."

"They're not headed toward Vega?"

"No. And we don't know why."

Thiraka stepped away from his officers and crossed the bridge, heading toward the kalralahr.

As he neared the old one, Thiraka bowed his head and spoke in a low hiss of respect. "The Ulysses Corridor is clear. As you predicted, the door to Earth is open. But new difficulties have arisen."

Kalralahr Bokoth turned his long, pale head toward Thiraka. Bokoth's face looked battle-worn. He had lost an eye, and deep scars spread out from the gloomy socket. "Difficulties, Thiraka?"

"Yes. One of our surveillance stations—"

"I know." Bokoth stroked the long, fine hairs on his chin and smiled, as though over Thiraka's surprise. "I'm having all intelligence routed directly to my cabin."

"Kalralahr, this is my ship. I've paid you tribute enough in turning over command of the battle group. All intelligence will be routed to the bridge."

Bokoth's good eye widened. "I wondered how long I could push you before you would behave honorably and defend yourself. There's hope for you after all. Now then, let me address your supposed difficulties. Yes, it's unfortunate that the humans have learned so soon of our attack on Pegasus. But that doesn't matter. By the time that merchantman reaches the *Tiger Claw*, our lead will be too great for them to intercept. If by some small miracle they do reach us, we will finish them as efficiently as we destroyed Pegasus. One carrier is no match for this battle group. Even the lowest of born can recognize that."

"But answer this: Why is the merchantman not headed to Vega sector? Doesn't that puzzle you?"

"It does." Bokoth turned his head toward the lift doors as they closed behind a human wearing an atmospheric suit.

"Where's the celebration?" the hairless ape asked, its voice sounding tinny through the translator attached to its suit. "The door to Earth is open. And you have your prize."

As the human drew closer, Thiraka noticed a silver cross hanging around the man's neck. He recognized that cross from history holos he had been forced to watch during his training. It represented a clan of humans known as Pilgrims.

"The NAVCOM AI has been reconfigured to your jump drives," the ape continued.

"Excellent. Now answer me two questions," Bokoth said in his most demanding tone. "Why was the *Concordia* alerted of our attack so soon?"

"That, I'm afraid, was unavoidable. Next question?"

Bokoth growled. "Explain *unavoidable*."

"I think the word translates clearly."

Raising a paw and extending long, jagged nails, Bokoth said, "If I discover—"

"You're not in a position to threaten me—after what I've given you."

Slowly, Bokoth lowered his paw. "A merchantman has been ordered to alert the *Tiger Claw*. Why isn't it headed to Vega sector?"

"I don't know. I'd worry about that."

"If you're lying—"

"There you go again. Haven't I already expressed what I want?"

"Yes. Most clearly. You have betrayed your race on a scale unimaginable, Pilgrim."

"I've lived up to my part of our agreement. Live up to yours. Destroy Earth."

Bokoth stared long and hard at the traitor. At last, he nodded.

REQUISITIONED
MERCHANTMAN
DILIGENT

MARCH 15, 2654
2150 HOURS ZULU TIME

EN ROUTE TO
BEACON 147

Taggart's hatch stood slightly open, and Blair peeked through the crack. *If a man's quarters say a lot about the man, then this place isn't talking.* Taggart kept only the bare essentials: cot, nightstand, and wide, battered desk. Even the old gray walls were bare.

Taggart sat at the desk, looking at a collection of ancient star charts printed on real paper. A half-dozen of them lay rolled up and bound by rubber bands at his elbow, along with his coffee mug. "Come in, Mr. Blair."

Blair entered and suddenly felt strange standing in this most personal of places. He blurted out, "We're holding steady on the beacon. Marshall has the helm." He neared the desk and ran his finger over one of the charts. "These must be antiques."

"Yeah," Taggart said. "They were made by the first explorers in the sector. Pilgrims."

"How did you get them?"

Taggart rolled up one of the maps. "Now that's a story too long to hear."

"I, uh, before . . . I couldn't help noticing the tattoo on your neck."

"What about the Pilgrim cross you hide under your shirt?"

Blair's hand went for the cross. Then, realizing he had betrayed himself, he thrust the hand to his side.

"Don't worry. We all have pasts. And secrets."

"It was my mother's."

"May I see it?"

Blair lifted the chain over his head and withdrew the cross. He handed it to Taggart, who ran his fingers slowly over the semicircle at the cross's top. The glimmer in his eyes grew brighter. He pressed the center symbol. A seven-inch blade shot out from the cross's bottom.

As he traced the blade with his index finger, he smiled again and said, "There was a time long ago when people looked up to the Pilgrims. They were at the forefront of space exploration. When I was a boy, I knew there was some kind of connection between God and the stars. I think the Pilgrims found that connection." He touched the plate again, retracting the blade, then returned it to Blair.

"You know," Taggart continued, "since the Pilgrims were defeated, not a single new quasar has been charted."

Without warning, a sudden surge of acceleration sent Blair reaching for the desk. He caught the edge and balanced himself as Taggart's coffee mug fell and broke.

"That idiot!" Taggart screamed. He shot to his feet and stormed out of the cabin.

Blair followed close behind, only then realizing what Marshall had done.

As Taggart entered the bridge, he shouted, "Get up!"

Marshall quickly left the captain's chair and moved to the co-pilot's seat. "That caffeine's killing your attitude, man."

"Did you change course?"

"I just boosted the power. Why dog it when we can be at the beacon in an hour?"

"That beacon is marking a gravity well," Taggart said through clenched teeth.

Marshall gave Blair a nervous look.

Swinging the navigation computer in front of him, Taggart's fingers danced over the touchpad until a Heads Up Display lit before them. A green, flat grid rotated and glowed as data bars on each side filled with coordinates. The grid began folding inward, creating a strange, swirling spike.

Blair knew all too well what a gravity well could do to a Confed capital ship, let alone a rusty old transport.

Shoving the navigation computer back on its swingarm, Taggart slid another display forward, one that offered multiple views of space through the *Diligent*'s outside cameras. He chose the image from the centerline unit and adjusted the telescopic lens to bring a dim object, the gravity well, into focus. Asteroids and debris plunged into the well, as though into a whirlpool, and disappeared. The *Diligent* screamed toward the same future.

Taggart beat his knuckle upon a thruster control button, throwing Blair and Marshall forward as retros violently kicked in. "One cubic inch of that well exerts more gravitational force than Earth's sun," he barked at Marshall.

"I screwed up. I get that. Forget the physics lesson," Marshall responded.

Numbers appeared on Taggart's nav computer screen. He frowned at them and tapped in new ones. "Come on, come on," he said, driving himself harder. "If I don't realign our entry vector, we won't make the jump."

"And if we don't make the jump . . ." Marshall began.

"We die," Taggart finished.

"Have we reached the entry vector's point of no return yet?" Blair asked.

"Not yet," Taggart said, throwing a toggle to automatically stabilize the now-groaning transport. "She's reaching out for us. Hear that?"

The *Diligent*'s hull protested much louder, and the gravity well appeared like a shimmering black mouth. The ship's thrusters whined as they fought to obey Taggart's course corrections. Still, the well grew larger, more hungry, and the space distortions now seemed more like hands reaching for the ship. Blair shivered.

Taggart gestured to the viewport. "Well, ladies, meet Scylla, bane to sailors and monster of myth."

"What's a Scylla?" Marshall asked.

But Blair answered for Taggart. "Ulysses sailed between the whirlpool Charybdis and the island monster Scylla. She snatched six of his men and ate them."

"I didn't need to know that," Marshall moaned.

Shaking a finger at Scylla, Taggart said, "This beauty's got an even bigger appetite. Hold on."

Blair got to the navigator's seat behind Taggart and Marshall. The captain threw a pair of toggles, and a bank of afterburners kicked the *Diligent* onto her side. Blair clung to the arms of his seat as the ship continued to yaw. Every seam and conduit in the old transport begged for relief. Within a few seconds the tremors became so violent that Blair fell from his chair. Marshall lost his grip as well, and thumped to the floor beside Blair.

Still glued to his seat, Taggart continued adjusting the *Diligent*'s course. The transport slowly rolled upright, sending Blair and Marshall sliding. As the ship finally balanced and artificial gravity readjusted, Blair looked over Taggart's shoulder at the Heads Up Display, which now showed a digital glide path that took them along Scylla's edge.

"Broken your grip, old girl," Taggart said. "Better luck next time."

The *Diligent* now skipped closer to Scylla, avoiding her mouth but coming very close. Space looked blurry along the starboard side.

Marshall shook his head. "This isn't a normal gravity well. What is this thing?"

"This *thing* is a distortion in space-time," Taggart explained. "Pilgrims were the first to chart it."

"So why is it off-limits?" Marshall asked.

"Because it's unstable."

A warning light flashed on the navigation computer, accompanied by a rapid beeping. The HUD winked out. The *Diligent* suddenly shifted to starboard.

"Nav computer's off-line," Blair observed.

"It's the magnetic fields," Taggart said. "Blair. Take the helm."

"I've never made a jump before."

Taggart cocked a brow. "Now would be a good time to learn." He rushed toward the hatchway.

Blair focused on Scylla as she shifted to the center viewport. He shot a look toward the hatchway, where Taggart had pulled off a maintenance panel.

The gravity well now dominated all viewports, a starving queen at her banquet table. A pair of discarded oxygen canisters collided and exploded on their way into her stomach. Asteroids spun and broke apart, leaving trails of themselves across the whirlpool. Even a comet had strayed too close to Scylla's arms and now painted a streak across the watery blur of her body.

A proximity alarm blared, and a digital countdown at Marshall's station read 9, 8, 7—

"Uh, Captain?" Marshall called out.

"What?"

"Five seconds to jump."

"So?"

"So if you don't get the nav computer back on line, this unstable gravity well is going to pull us in—one molecule at a time."

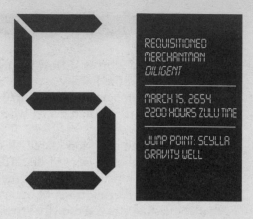

REQUISITIONED
MERCHANTMAN
DILIGENT

MARCH 15, 2654
2200 HOURS ZULU TIME

JUMP POINT: SCYLLA
GRAVITY WELL

Marshall shouted the final countdown: "Three, two . . ."

Blair glanced back at Taggart, who shoved a protein chip into place, then jiggled a wire.

"One!"

The navigation system snapped on, panels warming to their normal glow, coordinates spilling across four screens in front of Blair. *Snap*. Everything went dark.

Snap. Everything came back.

"Come on!" Marshall shouted.

After a tiny spark and loud hum, the instruments came back on. Blair read the coordinates and studied the course, but something deep inside said the computer was wrong. He couldn't explain the feeling, but he had felt it before during his training at the academy. The feeling tugged on his mind, his heart, and something even greater.

"Plot your course, Mr. Blair," Taggart said.

Mother? Father? Be with me now. Blair pulled out his cross and squeezed it. Then he obeyed the feeling as it told him to close his eyes. His fingers glided over the touchpad as though it were a musical instrument. Then he opened his eyes and stared at the upper left screen: COURSE PLOTTED.

Drawing in a long breath and holding it, Blair steered the *Diligent* into the gravity well.

Marshall released a long howl over the rattling consoles and conduits.

One, two, three, and the *Diligent* pierced the barrier—

And with eyes wide open, Blair could only see darkness. He cried out to Marshall. The other pilot did not answer. Then Blair realized that he hadn't heard himself call out, that all of his senses had been shut down, replaced by . . .

The feeling.

Never had he felt it so strongly, a connection to the universe that made no sense, that made perfect sense. His body had never belonged to him in the first place. It had always belonged to the universe. He understood at least that much of the feeling now.

The *Diligent*'s bridge reappeared as quickly as it had vanished. But life still hung between seconds. Taggart stood frozen on his way toward the bridge. Marshall leaned back in his chair, in mid-scream. And Blair somehow observed this while feeling as though he could move his body but realizing that he could not.

With a white-hot flash, the *Diligent* broke free from Scylla's arms and plunged back into normal space. Marshall finished his scream. Taggart came onto the bridge.

The return left Blair feeling empty, as though he had forgotten part of himself and needed to head back.

Taggart examined the nav computer's display. He opened his mouth, looked at Blair, started to say something, then just stared.

Feeling nervous over Taggart's odd look, Blair asked, "What happened?"

The captain held back a laugh. "You just plotted a jump through a gravity well in under five seconds. A NAVCOM can't do that." His gaze lowered to Blair's chest.

Seeing this, Blair gripped his cross for a moment before slipping it under his shirt. "I guess I just felt something."

"You didn't use the nav computer's trajectory. Why?"

"I don't know."

"Who cares how he did it," Marshall said. "That was one hell of a rocket ride. Not bad for the second-best pilot at the academy."

"Shut up," Taggart barked, turning to Marshall. "The next time you fail to follow my orders, I'll dump you with the rest of the garbage. You read me, Lieutenant?"

Tensing, Marshall kept his gaze forward and replied, "Yes, sir. I read you clearly, sir."

Satisfied that Marshall had been duly reprimanded, Taggart redirected his attention. "Plot a course for the *Tiger Claw*, Mr. Blair."

"Yes, sir."

Taggart rubbed his eyes, sighed loudly, then walked off the bridge.

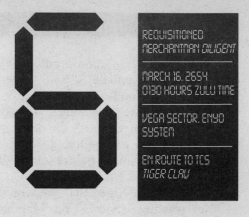

REQUISITIONED
MERCHANTMAN *DILIGENT*

MARCH 16, 2654
0130 HOURS ZULU TIME

VEGA SECTOR, ENYO
SYSTEM

EN ROUTE TO TCS
TIGER CLAW

Blair steered the *Diligent* down toward the great capital ship *Tiger Claw*. The *Claw*, as some called her, was shaped like a long, gray cylinder that had been split in two then glued on to a rectangular structure that was her runway and hangar bay. Inside the bay was the flight deck where small ships were berthed and repaired, and that was where Blair landed.

Five minutes later, Blair and Marshall left the *Diligent* and were checked in by two Confed Marines. After that, Blair suggested that they wait for Taggart to at least say good-bye.

"Now that," Marshall said, "is humorous."

Blair dropped his duffel. "I'm waiting."

With a hand on his brow, Marshall paced for a moment, then slipped off his own duffel. "You're right. We should wait. I'm not finished with him."

After a sigh over Marshall's threat, Blair had a look around. Rows of starfighters and bombers stretched off into the distance. The strong smell of heated metal, jet fuel, hydraulic fluid, and burning rubber hung heavily in the air, despite the best efforts of the ship's recyclers. While civilians would crinkle their noses at the smell, Blair smiled. *I'm home.* He touched a bulkhead next to the lift doors and came upon a patch welded there. Then he noticed dozens of other patches. "You've seen a lot of action," he whispered. "Guess you'll see a lot more."

"Hey, what are you doing?" someone familiar asked.

Blair turned in Taggart's direction. "Waiting for you. Just wanted to say thanks for the lift."

The captain paused before them. "Well, gentlemen, don't think I haven't enjoyed your company."

Marshall bore his teeth. "We won't. *Sir*."

Not wasting a second on Marshall, the captain focused on Blair. "I'm headed for the lift over there," he said, tipping his head toward the doors fifty meters away. "See you. And good luck."

Lifting his duffel, Blair said, "I'll walk with you."

"I won't," Marshall said.

Blair hurried after the captain. "Marshall? I'll meet you back here." He didn't wait for the expected reply and finally caught up with Taggart. "Before you go, tell me about your tattoo."

"You know what it is?" Taggart asked, lifting his voice over the whine of power tools.

"I think I got it figured out. It's a Kilrathi marker. You were a prisoner of war."

"I was on the *Iason* when they took her."

That caught Blair off guard. "The *Iason*? She was the first ship to have contact with the Kilrathi. You served under Commander Andropolos?"

Taggart nodded. "We encountered a spacecraft of unknown origin, transmitted a wide-band, nonverbal greeting, and waited. Four hours later she fired upon us with all batteries. But you know the story."

"Yeah. And I know there weren't supposed to be any survivors from the *Iason*."

"I guess not."

They reached the lift doors, which slid apart. Taggart stepped inside and turned around.

"Why don't you have it removed?" Blair asked, staring at the captain's tattoo.

"Let's just say it helps me remember."

"Remember what?"

"Why I fight."

The doors began to close.

Blair stepped forward. "Wait. I've seen photos and holos, but what do the Kilrathi look like? I mean, in the flesh?"

"They're ugly. Good luck."

The doors sealed.

"Right," Blair muttered, then hurried back to the other lift, where he found Marshall staring at a blonde tech whose smooth skin seemed out of place with her greasy coveralls. She stood beneath a Broadsword bomber, taking apart one of its mass driver cannons with a power wrench.

"I don't see the XO," Marshall said.

"I can see why."

"Maybe she can help." He strutted toward the woman, his boots barely touching the deck.

Blair rolled his eyes, then wandered toward a row of Rapier starfighters. He came to the first fighter, number thirty-five. He pictured himself in the cockpit, diving onto an enemy ship's tail, locking target, and—

He fought off a chill and lifted a computer slate from a rolling tool cart. The slate showed the fighter's mission status. Her next pilot had yet to be assigned. Not bothering to read more, Blair set down the slate and hurried up the cockpit ladder. He made sure that no one watched, then climbed into the cockpit.

Although the instrument panels were dark, he could easily imagine the left Visual Display Unit reporting battle damage, the right VDU showing options for the vidcom system and the targeting screen. The circular radar display, just left of center, showed a wave of red blips above him. "Break and attack," he told his ghostly wingman.

"Two Dralthis on your tail—one above, one below."

Blair felt a jolt in his gut, then looked down toward the person who had spoken. She stood nearly as tall as he and was about his age, maybe a little older. Her shoulder-length hair was a deep brown laced with gold curls. The shadows beneath her eyes and streak of lubricant on her cheek did not take away her beauty.

However, the oil-stained disposable plasticine coveralls she wore weren't very fashionable. With a socket wrench in one hand, an x-ray scanner in the other, she raised a thin brow and continued: "You've got five, maybe ten seconds—the clock is ticking. What do you do?"

"Simple. I go vertical and inverted, do a one-eighty at full throttle, apply the brakes, and drop in behind them."

"Bang. You're dead. Not fast enough. Dralthis are too quick—particularly in a climb. You've just taken a missile up your tailpipe."

Blair felt surprised by her tone. No lower-ranked tech had ever spoken to him this way. What did she hope to prove?

"Okay. Reverse the situation," she said. "You're locked on a Dralthi. It goes evasive, enters an asteroid belt. Clock is ticking."

With a loud snort, Blair pointed ahead. "I'm locked on. There's such thing as evasive because—"

"Bang. Dead again. It's an ambush. Five or six fighters hide behind rocks the size of your swollen head and pounce you."

An intense heat washed into Blair's face, and he balled his hands into fists.

She set down her tools and began untying her coveralls. "What's the matter? Did I bruise your ego?"

"No. I'm just not used to getting combat tips from a grease monkey."

As the words left Blair's mouth, he saw her step out of the coveralls to reveal her blood-red flight suit. "I'm Lieutenant Commander Jeanette Deveraux—your wing commander. You have a name, *nugget?*"

Blair straightened and saluted her, not that his after-the-fact respect would mean anything. "Lieutenant Christopher Blair, ma'am."

"Well, Lieutenant, if you want to play at being a fighter pilot, I suggest you find a virtual fun zone. Meanwhile, step down from the Rapier."

Feeling as though his face would burst into flames, Blair rose and set foot on the cockpit ladder. As he descended, he noticed the pilot's name in bright yellow letters along the pit's edge: LT.

COMMANDER VINCE "BOSSMAN" CHEN. Twenty-six Kilrathi paws representing kills had been set in neat rows beside the name, a scorch mark slashing through them. "Ma'am, the mission slate said this fighter was unassigned. I apologize. I didn't realize it was Bossman's."

"Who?"

"Lieutenant Commander Chen. Bossman." Blair gazed back at the Rapier. Had he read the name correctly? Yes, he had.

Deveraux's face creased even more.

Puzzled, Blair crossed to the tool cart and lifted the computer slate. "If this fighter's not his, then who got these twenty-six kills?"

She wrenched the slate from his hand. "What are you doing on the flight deck, anyway?"

"Looking for the XO," Marshall said, arriving at Blair's side.

Shifting her gaze to the far end of the flight deck, Deveraux nodded to a tall officer. "You found him." She turned on her heels and walked away.

UNITED
CONFEDERATION
CARRIER *TIGER CLAW*

MARCH 16, 2654
0200 HOURS ZULU TIME

VEGA SECTOR, ENYO
SYSTEM

Blair set foot on the bridge of the *Tiger Claw,* the largest ship he had ever served on. He could barely contain his excitement. Viewports wrapped around the bridge, the synthoglass so clear it seemed nothing stood between people and the vacuum. Dozens of officers and noncoms sat at dozens of consoles. Instrument panels at the radar, navigation, communications, tactical, and flight deck stations glowed in a rainbow of colors. Six holographic projectors shaped like upside-down domes hung from the ceiling, and one of them at the tactical radar board to Blair's left displayed a real-time, grid-enhanced image of six Hornets launching for patrol to replace the Rapiers now returning.

Captain Jay Sansky stood below the hologram, speaking with a radar officer and pointing to coordinates marking the fighter patrol's flight. Sansky was a middle-aged man who seemed friendly, unlike Commander Gerald.

With few words, Gerald had escorted Blair and Marshall to the bridge. Yes, the commander had identified himself, but Blair didn't even know Gerald's first name, and the man obviously liked it that way. He had looked angry over having to meet them on the flight deck. XOs typically don't greet new pilots or give them the welcome-aboard tour. That was the wing commander's job. But according to Gerald, Captain Taggart had called ahead to make sure that the XO served as escort. In an attempt to make Gerald feel better, Blair had explained the importance of the minidisc he now carried. Gerald had seemed unimpressed. And he had even forced Marshall to stay in the corridor, since Marshall had "no business on the bridge."

Not waiting for the commander to do an uninspired job of introducing him, Blair crossed to Captain Sansky, stood at attention, and gave a crisp salute that the captain returned. "First Lieutenant Christopher Blair reporting for duty, sir."

"At ease, Lieutenant." Sansky scrutinized Blair for a moment, then said, "I understand you have something for me."

"Yes, sir." He withdrew the minidisc from an inner breast pocket and handed it to Sansky. "An encrypted communiqué—from Admiral Tolwyn."

Sansky scratched his forehead and stared at the disc. "Why didn't the admiral send a drone from Pegasus?"

Blair cleared his throat, and his tone grew sad. "Sir. Pegasus was destroyed by a Kilrathi battle group seventeen hours ago. I'm sorry, sir."

The captain looked thoughtfully at Gerald, then crossed toward a wall of consoles, holding up the disc and shouting, "Communications. I want this decrypted ASAP."

"Aye-aye, sir," a young comm officer said, pivoting in his chair to accept the disc.

"If there's nothing else, sir?" Blair asked as Sansky returned.

"We don't kill the messenger anymore, Lieutenant. Instead, I'll just say welcome aboard. And dismissed."

Drawing up his shoulders, Blair saluted and turned to go.

"Hey, Lieutenant," Gerald called. "You wouldn't be related to Arnold Blair, would you?"

Steeling himself, Blair looked back and answered, "He was my father, sir."

Gerald nodded, his lips rising in a self-satisfied grin that suddenly fell. "He married a Pilgrim woman, didn't he?"

"Yes, sir. My father married a Pilgrim, sir."

"Mixed marriages seldom work out." The commander shifted in front of Blair, his face a cold, dark knot. "Pilgrims don't think like us."

Blair returned the icy look. "You won't have to worry, sir. They're both dead."

Sansky placed a hand on the commander's shoulder. "I'm sure the lieutenant's ancestry will have no bearing on his performance, Mr. Gerald."

"No, sir. I'm sure it won't."

"That's all, Lieutenant," Sansky said, obviously growing weary of his refereeing. "I suggest you stow your gear and take the virtual tour. Your onboard accounts have already been set up. You'll find hard copies of everything in the personnel department."

Blair nodded. "Thank you, sir."

In the corridor outside, Blair stormed silently past Marshall. He suddenly felt trapped in who he was, cheated out of a fair life. All of the hard work, the training, the studying, the suffering—all of it—for nothing. *I'm a Pilgrim half-breed. That's all I am. None of you can see past that.*

"Hey, hey, hey," Marshall said. He ran up behind Blair and yanked him around. "What? Are you having a moment?"

Blair mouthed a curse, stared teary-eyed at the deck, then said, "It never changes."

"Look, I overheard a little of that. Forget Gerald. Let it go. Because right now, we're about to meet our fellow pilots. The men and women we're going to fight with, perhaps even die with, and perhaps—"

"Don't worry, Marshall. I won't let the fact that I'm upset keep you from getting a date."

"Me? I'm worried about it keeping *you* from getting a date. You watch the old Marshall man in action. I'll teach you how to make friends." Marshall threw his arm over Blair's shoulder and led him down the corridor.

By the time they reached the pilots' mess, Blair's rage had cooled to a simmer. Marshall pushed open the hatch, and Blair followed him inside.

Considering the large number of pilots stationed aboard the *Tiger Claw*, Blair had thought the mess would be spacious and well-equipped. It was anything but.

Two pilots played chess on a scratched-up old board. One of them, a tall, sturdy man with a high-and-tight crew cut and Roman nose, smiled to make the long scar on his face twist a little. He took the other pilot's pawn and laughed. "You're going down, Forbes."

"Mr. Polanski. It's good to know you still dream." Forbes, a beautiful, dark-skinned woman who had cut her hair short and dyed it blonde, stared at the board for a moment, then quickly made a move, took Polanski's bishop, and grinned.

The chess players noticed their entrance, as did the half-dozen other pilots seated at tables, eating and sipping drinks. Blair gave a quick nod hello.

But Marshall marched into the room like a grand marshal at a Confederation victory parade. "Hey! How's everybody doing? Lieutenant Todd Marshall."

Silence. Dead silence. Blair swore he could hear molecules bumping against each other. He scanned the blank faces of the pilots and felt his breath shorten. A few returned to their conversations.

Not bothered by their reaction, Marshall went on. "I'd like you all to meet a close personal friend, Lieutenant Christopher Blair—who just happens to be the second-best pilot on this hunk of junk."

Several of the pilots now looked up. One with reddish-brown hair and long sideburns removed the cigar stub from his mouth and spoke in an Australian accent. "Who you calling the best, nugget?"

Blair leaned toward Marshall. "So this is the secret to your overwhelming popularity?"

Marshall took a step toward the cigar-smoking pilot, who quickly stood. "There's two ways to figure out who's the best," he said as he read the pilot's nametag. "One way, Captain St. John, involves you trying to kick my butt—"

St. John frowned, having no idea what to make of Marshall. Blair knew the feeling all too well.

"What's the other way?" St. John asked.

Marshall smiled—a very dangerous look now. "The other way? Why that involves my other close personal friend. Mr. Johnnie Walker Black." After quickly unzipping a pouch on his duffel, Marshall produced a bottle of Scotch, very good Scotch, the rare, real stuff. Now Marshall commanded the room.

Turning toward Forbes, St. John spoke her name as a question, as though she were the group's unofficial leader.

Keeping her gaze trained on the bottle, Forbes said, "We're on stand-down. One won't hurt."

Marshall moved quickly to a shelf, fetched a plastic glass, and poured one for Forbes. "This might even help."

The other pilots flocked around Marshall, who looked at Blair with an I-told-you-so expression plastered on his face.

Standing in the chart room with the hatch sealed, Captain Sansky and Commander Gerald waited as the computer booted up and prepared to play the decoded message delivered by Lieutenant Blair. Sansky had already guessed what Admiral Tolwyn would ask of him, and he knew that he could not disobey orders at this time. He had, on more than one occasion, disagreed with the admiral, but too much was at stake now. Responsibility would rest upon the admiral's shoulders, and it felt good to be someone else's instrument.

Finally, the monitor showed Admiral Tolwyn standing on the *Concordia*'s bridge. "Jay, I'll be brief. The Kilrathi took Pegasus. They have her NAVCOM AI. By the time this communication reaches you, they will be approximately thirty-five hours from the Charybdis jump point and Earth. Confed capital ships are headed home now. The *Concordia* battle group will be there in approximately thirty-seven hours. I'm ordering the *Tiger Claw* to the Charybdis Quasar. You are to use any means necessary to gather information as to the Kilrathi whereabouts, capacity, and plan of attack. I need intelligence, old friend. Use Taggart. He knows Vega sector better than any man alive—he can get you to Charybdis quickly. Good luck. Tolwyn out."

"Sir, I don't like it," Gerald said. "The disc came to us on the *Diligent*, entrusted to a Pilgrim half-breed."

"Your reservations have been duly noted. Now then. Send for Taggart."

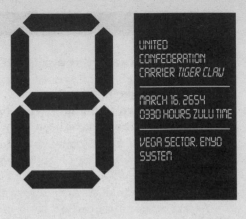

UNITED
CONFEDERATION
CARRIER *TIGER CLAW*

MARCH 16, 2654
0330 HOURS ZULU TIME

VEGA SECTOR, ENYO
SYSTEM

Blair settled into a chair and watched Forbes and Polanski play another chess game. Marshall held the bottle of Scotch and wandered over to observe the competition.

The youngest of four sons, Marshall had grown up in a competitive household where his brothers had constantly challenged him. Those challenges had made him a great pilot.

But to look at Marshall now, you'd never think he was capable of flying. He could barely stand as he drew closer to the chess game. "Take his pony with your castle," he told Forbes, then took a swig from the bottle.

She moved her "castle" and captured Polanski's "pony." Then she folded her arms over her chest. "Check."

"Where?" Polanski challenged.

"Mate," Marshall said.

"No way," Polanski said in realization. "That's cheatin'."

Forbes gave Marshall a penetrating stare. "So there's a brain behind that mouth?"

Marshall flashed one of his trademark smiles. He poured her another drink, and she stood. For a second, her gaze met Blair's, and he turned away.

"Your friend always this talkative?" she asked Marshall.

"He just made the fatal error of mistaking Commander Deveraux for your average grease monkey."

She circled to face Blair and bent down to his level. "What happened?"

Blair squirmed as he realized that everyone in the room now watched him. "All I did was sit in Lieutenant Commander Chen's fighter."

Smiles faded. Polanski shifted away.

Captain St. John looked up from his Scotch. "Who?"

"Lieutenant Commander Chen. Bossman."

The cigar came out. "Bossman? Anybody here know a Bossman?"

"No," someone said.

"Never heard of him," someone else added.

Shooting to his feet so quickly that he knocked over his chair, Blair said, "What's with you people?" The coldness in their faces angered him. Was this how they treated their dead friends?

A big black man with a widow's peak and a nametag that read Knight moved to Blair, his expression calm, his voice nearly a whisper. "Leave it alone, Blair."

"Leave what alone?"

"You're asking after a man who never existed," St. John said.

"I'm pretty sure he did."

It all happened in a moment as blurry as Scylla. One nanosecond St. John sat before his drink, the next he stood and pushed Blair hard in the chest. "He never existed," St. John corrected. "Now, I suggest you change the subject. Or I'll change it for you."

Marshall threaded his way through the other pilots and came up behind St. John. "You have a problem with my friend?"

"That's right. I do."

"Then you have a problem with me."

St. John whirled around. "Oh, yeah. You're going to love this—"

Expecting St. John to rush Marshall, Blair tensed, preparing to leap on the man's back.

But the pilot whirled back to him, grabbed his shirt, and drove him into the bulkhead.

Marshall employed Blair's original strategy and leapt on St. John's back, slinging an arm under the man's chin.

Likewise, Polanski slipped his arm around Marshall's neck and began prying Marshall away.

As St. John's hands got yanked back, Blair's shirt tore open to expose his cross.

"He's a Pilgrim!" St. John cried, then released Blair, who had suddenly become a live wire.

Everyone in the mess stared at the cross. Marshall cursed and pounded the bulkhead. The pilots closest to the hatch shifted back, blocking the exit.

Forbes elbowed her way through the others to get a closer look at the pariah named Christopher Blair. "Excuse me?"

"If you ladies don't stand down, you're going to have a problem with me." Blair knew who had said that, but he couldn't see her past the others. Good. She also couldn't see him. Using his temporary cover, he slid his cross beneath his shirt as the pilots snapped to attention.

"I want an explanation. Hunter?" Deveraux asked, calling St. John by his call sign.

But before the man could answer, Blair hurried forward to address Lieutenant Commander Deveraux. "Hunter and the others were just making Lieutenant Marshall and me feel at home, ma'am."

She stared suspiciously at him, then at St. John. "Lieutenant?"

The captain gave Blair a slight glance and said, "Uh, that's right, Lieutenant, ma'am."

Blair couldn't hide his dark feelings. "There, you see, ma'am? I guess this conversation *never existed*." He bolted through the open hatch.

In the dimly lit and silent chart room, Captain Sansky looked up to consider the red dots on the ghostly tactical schematic that Lieutenant Commander Obutu had pulled up for him. Those holographic dots moved toward the broad limbs of the Charybdis Quasar. Behind the quasar, a single yellow line stretched toward a floating Earth.

The hatch opened, and Gerald stepped inside. Captain James Taggart followed, lifting a hand to cover a yawn. "Captain Sansky. From one captain to another—never wake up a tired sailor unless we're talking life-or-death situation."

"Then let's talk, Mr. Taggart."

Moving beneath the holograph, Taggart stared at the Kilrathi battle group arrowing toward the quasar. "They're in a hurry," he muttered.

"I know *of* you, Taggart, but I'm afraid I don't know you. You're a civilian captain flying a requisitioned transport, yet you come to me with classified orders from Admiral Tolwyn."

Taggart smirked. "And you don't trust me, Blair, or the disc."

"Would you?"

"No."

Sansky nodded to the holograph. "This tactical schematic outlines a nightmare, Mr. Taggart. It tells me that the Kilrathi have a NAVCOM, and with it, the capacity to jump into Earth space. Based on that nightmare, I must take radical action that, if it and you are a lie, could compromise this ship, her crew, and Earth— all of which are unacceptable. Before I put my command in harm's way, I must be certain that you and the orders you bear are legitimate." Sansky reached into his breast pocket and produced the decoded disc. "So, I ask you, Mr. Taggart, what proof do you have that this is authentic?"

Taggart reached into his inner vest pocket and withdrew a small, shiny object. He tossed it to Sansky, who caught and quickly examined it. Between his fingers rested a gold class ring, its surfaces worn, its emerald dull. Sansky held it to the holograph's light and read the inscription: ANNAPOLIS NAVAL ACADEMY, 1941. He closed his now trembling hand over the ring and stared with disbelief at Taggart. "How did you get this?"

"Tolwyn gave it to me eight months ago. He thought it might be useful in situations like getting a captain to follow his orders."

Gerald crossed to Sansky and gestured to see the ring. Sansky handed it to him, then turned to the intercom. "Con. Plot a course for the Charybdis Quasar, full speed."

Lieutenant Commander Obutu shifted from the tactical

schematic console to read the navigator's coordinates on another screen. Obutu, an earnest black man, tough as titanium, with a thick brow and a face that seemed regularly haunted by a past of which he would not speak, remained a comfort and a mystery to Sansky. As the lieutenant commander further surveyed the screen, a query creased his face. "Sir, the nearest jump point to Charybdis is four days hard travel from our present position. How are we supposed to get there in time?"

"There's a class two pulsar eleven hours from here," Taggart said. "We can jump there."

Obutu began a rapid-fire sequence of key commands, then looked to Sansky. "Not on the charts, sir. NAVCOM does not have those coordinates."

"I have them," Taggart said.

"No one's jumped a pulsar for forty years," Gerald pointed out, eyeing Taggart with an ugly look. "And even then, they were Pilgrims."

"I don't believe we have a great deal of choice, Mr. Gerald," Sansky fired back. "If the battle is to be decided at Charybdis, then we have to be there." He regarded Taggart. "Plot your course."

With a nod, Taggart headed for a navigation subterminal.

Swearing under his breath, Gerald moved close to Sansky, out of Taggart's earshot. "Sir. This ring means nothing." He returned the antique to Sansky. "You shouldn't—"

"This ring has been in Tolwyn's family for sixteen generations. Any man who carries it has the admiral's full confidence."

"If it's real—which it may not be—then I can't believe Tolwyn gave it to a civilian."

"Believe it. And you have your orders. Prepare for jump."

As Gerald saluted and left, Sansky watched Taggart, wishing he could see past the man's mysteries.

Life had become far more interesting. And dangerous.

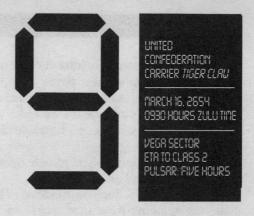

UNITED
CONFEDERATION
CARRIER *TIGER CLAW*

MARCH 16, 2654
0930 HOURS ZULU TIME

VEGA SECTOR
ETA TO CLASS 2
PULSAR: FIVE HOURS

With the lights off and his eyes closed, Blair lay on his cot in the quarters he now shared with Marshall. He needed to sleep. Needed to dream. Dream about anyplace but the carrier. He thought of dreams he would like to have, dreams of home, of Nephele, of his aunt and uncle who had worked so hard to raise him after his parents had died. He thought of old girlfriends, of old summer jobs, of a particular July 17 birthday party that had marked the end of his teenage years. He considered his time at the academy on Hilthros, days that felt like a million years ago. His life had become a streak of indistinct memories. Nothing stood out anymore. The only thing real was the Pilgrim cross around his neck. A blessing. A curse.

How did I get here? I was just a kid who liked to wrestle and was raised on a farm. I joined up to get flying experience, not to become another Confederation statistic. I remember my uncle telling me never to join the service. What has it done for me? What has it really done for me?

The lights snapped on. Covering his eyes, Blair sat up. He heard a shuffling of boots, a zipper being pulled up, and the rattle of metal on metal. He squinted and saw Marshall standing in a crimson flight suit, his battered helmet tucked in the crook of his arm.

"We going out?" Blair asked.

"No. Just me. I pulled security with Lieutenant Forbes."

"So why did you wake me up?"

Marshall shook his index finger at Blair's cross and opened his mouth.

But Blair beat him to the punch. "So I changed my mind. But I can't change who I am."

"No, you can't. But you made a promise back at the academy that you wouldn't wear that anymore. I'm not saying to throw it away. I think you know what I'm saying."

"It brings me luck, Todd."

"It's going to get you killed—*Chris*."

Blair took the cross in hand, as though to protect it. "I was wearing this when I made the jump. You heard Taggart. A NAV-COM can't do what I did."

"That had nothing to do with luck. It was about training and desire." Marshall reached toward Blair. "Take it off."

Drawing back, Blair held the cross tightly against his chest. "It's who I am. Or who I should be."

"You know what? You really messed up this time. And now you need someone watching your back. But I can't always be there."

"I don't expect that from anyone—especially you."

"Oh, man," Marshall said, turning away. "You're going to get whacked. If not by the Kilrathi, then—"

"This is getting old."

Marshall collapsed on his cot, smoothed back his hair, then rubbed his bloodshot eyes. "I'm trying to have a sensitive moment. I don't know why I bother." He sprang up and left.

Blair fell back on his cot. Then an idea suddenly made him sit up. "Merlin. Activate."

The little man yawned and walked along the edge of a storage locker opposite the cot. "What time is it?"

"The Pilgrims. What can you tell me about them?" Blair crawled to the edge of the cot.

"I'm afraid I have very little on the Pilgrims. Your father wiped my flash memory."

"Don't you have anything? A temp file you forgot to erase?"

"I'm sorry, Christopher."

Blair stood and crossed to the latrine. He leaned over the sink for a few minutes, splashing warm water on his face. He eventually looked to the mirror, but his dark hair and dusky skin remained blurred by condensation. After drying off, he opened his locker door and withdrew a clean uniform.

"Where are you going?" Merlin asked.

"To talk to someone who may know more about the Pilgrims."

After twenty minutes of travel, Blair found the hatch he had been looking for and touched the bell key.

"Come."

The door automatically opened, and Blair entered to admire Captain Taggart's spacious accommodations and bunk with thick mattress and comforter.

"Except for a few specs of light, it's all emptiness," Taggart said, standing at a large viewport. "If it were up to me, I'd let the Kilrathi have it all—just leave Earth alone."

"Sir? We need to talk."

"I've been in a thousand different solar systems, and I've never seen anything in the void as beautiful as our own sun breaking through the clouds after a rainstorm . . ." Taggart turned from the viewport. "What is it, Lieutenant?"

Blair crossed to a well-padded chair and took a seat. "All my life I've been put down for being part Pilgrim—and I barely know why. Most people don't want to talk about it or don't really know why humans and Pilgrims hated each other so much."

"That's right. Most people don't like to talk about it."

"C'mon. You know about them. Tell me the long story about how you got the star charts. Have you ever met a real Pilgrim—not a half-breed like me? What are they like? What about the war? What do you know?"

"You're one of the last descendants of a dying race," Taggart said. "Pilgrims were the first human space explorers and settlers. For five centuries they defied the odds. They embraced space and were rewarded with a gift: a flawless sense of direction. No computers, Blair. No compasses. No charts. They just knew. Then, in a small number, about one in a million, a change started to occur."

"What kind of change?"

"They learned to feel the magnetic fields created by black holes and quasars—to negotiate singularities. They learned to navigate not just the stars but space-time itself."

Blair shook as a powerful chill fanned across his shoulders. To *feel* the magnetic fields created by black holes and quasars. To navigate space-time itself. It seemed impossible. And possible. And in his blood. "So the Pilgrims could perform like a NAVCOM AI."

"You've got it backwards. The billions of calculations necessary to lead us through a black hole or quasar are the NAVCOM's recreation of the mind of a single Pilgrim."

He nodded in wonder. "How did the war start?"

Taggart moved back to the window, and as he did so, Blair saw his lips come together and his eyes get teary. "You spend so much time out here alone, you end up losing your humanity. The Pilgrims began to lose touch with their heritage. They saw themselves as superior to humans. And in their arrogance, they chose to abandon all things human in order to follow their destiny. Some say they believed they were gods, others that they were angels."

"You believe they were gods?"

"No. But I do believe they were touched by God." He looked back, his eyes still glassy. "And like it or not, you've got some of that inside you."

Blair's people had done great things. And terrible things. Had they been gods? Demons? Where was the line? And now that he knew his heritage, where did he go from here? For every question answered, it seemed Taggart had raised three more. Blair simply wanted to ask, "So how do I live like this? What kind of life should I expect?" But the captain did not have the answers. No one did. Except Blair.

Taggart sighed and said, "I have to get to the bridge. We'll be jumping in a few hours. I'd like you to be there."

"I will." He ambled toward the window. "You mind if I stay here a while?"

"No. Just don't drink my coffee."

Blair grinned, then listened to him leave.

Something flashed at the corner of his eye. Two patrolling Rapiers in tight formation pierced the night. Behind them, far in the distance, lay an enormous, flashing gulf that Blair recognized as a pulsar, a spinning, superdense mass of particles called neutrons. Blair wondered how many of his forefathers had jumped here.

And he wondered how many other Pilgrims were still out there, considering their future among the stars.

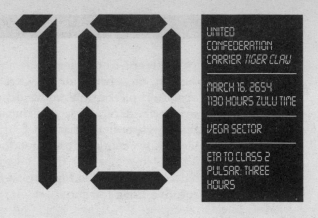

UNITED
CONFEDERATION
CARRIER *TIGER CLAW*

MARCH 16, 2654
1130 HOURS ZULU TIME

VEGA SECTOR

ETA TO CLASS 2
PULSAR: THREE
HOURS

First Lieutenant Todd Marshall grinned so hard that it hurt. He accelerated ahead of Lieutenant Forbes's Rapier, leaving her in the storm of his thruster wash.

Dialing up the rear turret view, Marshall watched as Forbes expertly recovered, kicked in her afterburners, and burst toward him like an angry hawk. "This is a security patrol, nugget," she said sternly. "Unauthorized maneuvers will not be tolerated. You'd better get with—or out of—the program." Her Rapier settled in beside his.

Five thousand kilometers ahead sat an indistinct pocket of space designated as nav point one, the first of three stops on their grand security tour of nothingness. Marshall activated navigation mode and glanced at the white cross-hairs on his radar scope and HUD. He adjusted course until the cross-hairs each floated in their centers. The rest of the radar display had been divided in four and would flash in the appropriate section when he took a missile or laser hit, not that he had seen that flash very often.

Sometimes he wished the Rapier's controls were more challenging. The Rapier was, after all, a very real fighter, not some funzone simulator used to zap computer-generated targets. Yet her controls were just as simple to operate. Then again, that simplicity gave him a heck of a lot more time to concentrate on whacking Kilrathi.

"Delta Two? I'm lined up," Forbes reported.

"Roger. Good light over here," he said, glancing at the autopilot display, the AUTO button now lit.

"Engage autopilot on my mark. Mark."

Marshall tapped the key and felt the powerful force of the Rapier's twin thrusters as they carried him toward the point.

In a few minutes, the Rapier slowed. The nav point lay just a klick ahead. He checked the radar. A single blue blip that represented Forbes's Rapier stood off to port, otherwise the zone remained clear. "Looks like we got zip here, Lieutenant. How boring is this?"

"Sometimes boring is good," she said.

Nav point two, a sprawling area of outer-space real estate that offered lovely views of more nothingness, came and went without enemy contact, as did nav point three. With the sweep completed, they started back for the carrier, passing the next security patrol pilots as they took their Rapiers out to new nav points and new heights of boredom.

Once the autopilot had disengaged at 2,200 kilometers out from the *Claw*, Forbes contacted the ship and requested clearance to land. They were put on standby. Marshall's eyelids grew heavy, and he longed for a shower, for his cot.

"Hey, Marshall. Did you know that women can outfly and outshoot men? We don't manhandle our instruments, and we do better at multitasking. We can keep track of four enemy fighters."

Marshall snapped from his doze. "Hey, it takes skill to handle four enemy fighters. It doesn't matter if you're a man or a woman." He glanced at the opening flight deck doors. "Watch this." Toggling to the flight boss's channel, he said, "This is Delta Two. Permission to land?"

The flight boss's beefy face clicked on the VDU. "Delta Two. You are cleared to land."

Tensing every muscle in his body, Marshall fired the afterburners and banked hard, lining up with the flight deck.

"Whoa, that must've been three G's," Forbes said sarcastically.

Taking his cue, Marshall cut the stick hard left and rolled as he gunned the throttle. "Try this." Upside-down, he raced down toward the runway.

"Delta Two. You're coming in too hot," the flight boss cried, his face a survey course in fear. "Abort. I repeat. Abort. Delta Two. Do you copy?"

But Marshall held course, gazing up at the runway, now his ceiling, as, in the distance, orange-suited insects made way. He approached the energy field between vacuum and atmosphere.

"Delta Two. YOU ARE INVERTED!"

"No. You are!" Marshall shouted back, then released a laugh. The Rapier vibrated sharply as it penetrated the energy barrier and roared into the hangar, a dampened echo in its wake.

"C'mon, man. You're inverted!"

"Not anymore," Marshall told the keen-eyed flight boss. He jammed the stick left and rolled upright.

But he had misjudged his speed. Even as he fired retros, he knew he would overshoot the runway by at least twenty, maybe even thirty meters.

And worse, dead ahead lay a fuel truck, strategically placed by God to punish one First Lieutenant Todd Marshall for goofing off.

Deckmaster Peterson ran across the runway and toward the fuel truck. He crossed in front of the vehicle, on his way to the driver's side. He spotted Marshall's fighter and looked horrified as he extended his arms across the truck's hood.

Marshall blasted toward him, retros wailing to the heavens, wings and fuselage rattling so violently that he thought the fighter would simply shatter across the deck before ever stopping.

Peterson screamed.

The Rapier slowed but kept moving.

Snap! Click! And Marshall got thrown forward, his harness digging into his shoulders. The retros dropped from their high pitch into a comforting, easy hum. The Rapier settled onto her landing skids to reveal Peterson, still clutching the truck. The deckmaster reached out with a shaky hand and touched the Rapier's nose cannon.

Marshall slid aside his HUD viewer, then unlatched his helmet and O$_2$ mask. Sweat drenched his face.

"I'll have your wings," the flight boss said, his eyes ablaze. "Wait until your wing leader . . ."

"What?"

The flight boss regarded something off camera, then shouted, "Delta One!"

Marshall's VDU switched to an image of Forbes in her cockpit. "Now what were you saying?"

He watched her sweep over the runway, her Rapier upside-down and at full throttle. She plowed through the energy field, killed the engines, then ignited retros to roll a full 540 degrees, righting herself at the last possible moment before touch-down. And she had not overshot the runway.

"Now that's how you do it," she shouted.

Marshall rushed out of his cockpit and toward her fighter. The flight crews kept their distance, not wanting to catch Marshall's highly contagious insanity.

Forbes's canopy popped, and she removed her mask to flash him a perfect grin.

"You did that to impress me," he said, leaving no room for the question.

"I guess so."

He stared at her, and in her eyes he found something they now shared, a passion for danger, for flying on the edge.

"You're a total maniac!" she said.

He saluted her. "Maniac Marshall at your service, ma'am."

They burst into laughter.

Then Forbes stiffened as she looked past him. "Oh, no."

Lieutenant Commander Deveraux stood fuming on the opposite side of the flight deck. She held her gaze a moment, then spun and stomped out.

Her silence left Marshall even more worried. "What happens now?"

Forbes looked to where Deveraux had been standing. "I'm not sure. I'm really not sure."

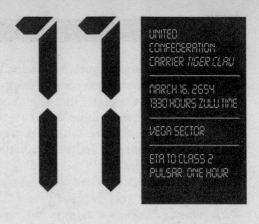

11

UNITED
CONFEDERATION
CARRIER *TIGER CLAW*

MARCH 16, 2654
1330 HOURS ZULU TIME

VEGA SECTOR

ETA TO CLASS 2
PULSAR: ONE HOUR

Back in her quarters, Lieutenant Commander Jeanette Deveraux keyed off the shower, wrapped herself in a towel, then found the chair at her small desk. She sat there, staring at the statue of the little dog, a Brussels griffon, that she had ordered from a Datanet catalog. The dog's short, bearded muzzle and blond fur reminded her of Pierre, a stray dog she had adopted as a child. She felt a kinship with that dog and had loved him for ten years before he had died. He lay buried in Belgium, behind the orphanage. *Sleep well, my dear Pierre. Sleep well.*

Her hatch bell rang. "Who is it?"

"Me."

"You don't want to be here right now."

"Just let me in. *Please.*"

Deveraux stood and shrugged. "You're at your own risk." She touched the keypad, and the hatch opened.

"Single malt . . . just for you," Forbes said, holding Lieutenant Todd Marshall's bottle of Scotch.

She glanced at the bottle, then shifted back to her chair but couldn't bring herself to sit. "Trying to bribe me? Well it won't work—especially with *his* liquor."

"I'm trying to thank you. The flight boss would've brought us up on charges if you hadn't said something."

"He told you we spoke?"

"Not exactly. But I could tell that you had already disarmed him. You're the only one on board who could do that. Raznick hates pilots. We get his flight deck dirty and raise his blood pressure. But you he respects."

"Do you know why?"

Her expression said that she didn't.

"Because I work with him. Not against him. That's simple math. No advanced degree required."

Forbes hid her gaze.

"What were you thinking?"

Biting her lower lip, Forbes stalled. "Well, I wasn't thinking with my head."

Deveraux beat a fist on her thigh. "Rosie, you'll get yourself killed doing that. How could you follow *that* kind of lead?"

"I don't know."

"Well, let me tell you something. I think—"

"I *know* what you're thinking."

"I think you're one of my best pilots. I can't afford to lose you."

And that lifted Forbes's head. "Sorry. I was just showing off a bit in front of Maniac."

"Maniac?"

"Lieutenant Marshall. He has a new call sign." Forbes went to a cabinet, removed a glass, and began pouring a drink.

"I hope it felt really good," Deveraux said, driving the point home but realizing that her tone had been too cruel.

"Actually, it felt great."

Forbes handed her the Scotch, and she took a healthy swig. "See that it never happens again."

"It won't."

Deveraux took another pull on her drink as her friend, now visibly relaxed, sat on the cot and yawned.

Then Forbes stared at her. Deveraux stared back. Forbes looked away, as did Deveraux. Then it all happened again.

"What?" Deveraux asked.

"I don't want to pry, but I've noticed you've been giving special attention to Maniac's friend . . ."

She lifted the towel higher over her chest. "Oh, really? I think that's your imagination working overtime."

"He's pretty cute," Forbes pointed out.

Seeing that her Scotch glass stood empty, Deveraux said, "Just shuddup and pour."

Forbes offered her a small amount, and with the lift of her brow, Deveraux gestured for a full glass.

Yes, she did see something in First Lieutenant Christopher Blair. And that was why it hurt so much.

12

UNITED
CONFEDERATION
CARRIER *TIGER CLAW*

MARCH 16, 2654
1415 HOURS ZULU TIME

VEGA SECTOR

ETA TO CLASS 2
PULSAR: FIFTEEN
MINUTES

Captain Jay Sansky sat at his desk in the welcome peace of his quarters. The antique clock hanging on the bulkhead above him ticked nearly in synch with the drums and violins of a classical song coming from his minidisc player. He had come here to meditate before the jump, to gather some thoughts while pushing others away.

In truth, he had come to bury the past.

He turned once more to the holopic, a framed, three-dimensional picture sitting on his desk. He smiled at the group of young men and women posed in crisp Naval Academy uniforms, their eyes full of hope, their expressions hard and filled with courage. Sansky had been with them that day, a young officer with a thin face and a full head of hair. Beside him stood Bill Wilson, former commander of Pegasus Station, now assumed dead. Bill wore his twisted grin proudly, and he had never betrayed his rebel's heart.

Lieutenant Commander Obutu's voice boomed over the intercom. "Captain Sansky? You're needed in the chart room."

"On my way."

Sansky stared a moment more at the holopic, at the two

young men with their whole lives ahead of them, two young men unaware of the fire that lay in their hearts. He replaced the holopic, opened a drawer, and lifted his hip flask. With an unsteady hand, he brought the flask to his lips and took several swigs before returning the whiskey. He started for the hatch, then hurried back to the desk, where he scooped up Tolwyn's ring.

Admiral Geoffrey Tolwyn had an unspoken agreement with the universe that allowed him to take tremendous risks. Perhaps carrying a piece of the admiral would allow Sansky to do the same.

As Blair stepped into the carrier's chart room, a huge holographic display swept up his attention. Stretching from deck to overhead, the semitransparent images drew long shadows across the walls and over the navigation subterminal where Taggart sat, keying in numbers and gazing at his screen.

A red blip designated by tiny letters as the *Tiger Claw* lay at the holograph's center. The blip flashed as it moved toward a constantly moving set of circles: a mathematical picture of the Class 2 pulsar. The databar beside the pulsar showed thousands of scrolling coordinates in space-time, coordinates being fed into the carrier's NAVCOM AI by Taggart.

"They told me you were here, sir," Blair said.

"Look at it, Lieutenant," Taggart suggested, still intent on his screen. "What do you see?"

Blair shrugged; wasn't it obvious? "That's a Class Two pulsar."

"Explain."

"Well, unlike a black hole, which is just one doorway, or a quasar, which has the potential of containing thousands of doorways, this pulsar has an infinite number of constantly changing doorways."

"Great. You remember your academy lessons. Now just look at it and read the map."

"I don't know what to say. Those doorways, they, uh, each one is capable of taking us to another part of the galaxy. The problem is, most of them are dead ends."

"With an emphasis on *dead*." Taggart swung around and cocked a brow.

The grid surrounding the *Tiger Claw* began to deform as a long spike pierced it, then gradually pulled itself inside out to form a tube with a thick, wide hole at its neck. Blair watched, fascinated, as the carrier stopped before the gap.

The chart room's hatch hissed open. Gerald and Lieutenant Commander Deveraux passed into the holograph's eerie glow. Blair craned his head, wanting to vanish into the shadows. Then he cringed as he heard Deveraux's voice. "Why aren't you at your station, Lieutenant?"

Blair faced them, their eyes like two pairs of muzzles, locked on target. "Ma'am, I—"

"I asked Lieutenant Blair to be here," Taggart cut in.

The hatch opened again.

"Why?" Gerald asked.

"I authorized it," Captain Sansky said, entering the room and double-timing toward Taggart. "Status?"

"Coordinates are laid in," Taggart said. "One keystroke to finish the upload." He went to holograph and let his finger follow a course across the wide gap in the quadrant. "The Ulysses Corridor. Four days hard travel using three known jump points. By using the pulsar, we'll be there in"—he glanced to a digital clock above his station—"less than three minutes."

"If your calculations are correct," Gerald said, grinding out the words.

Back at his console, Taggart touched the final key, finishing the upload. "They're right."

Gerald steered himself toward Taggart. "NAVCOM and the finest minds in the Confederation couldn't plot this jump. What makes you so sure you're right?"

A flicker of a grin wiped across Taggart's lips. "Because they're Pilgrim coordinates, Mr. Gerald."

"What?" Gerald's gaze swept back to the databar.

Taggart crossed into the big commander's line of sight. "We'll have a lovely view from the bridge."

◆   ◆   ◆

"Maniac" Marshall jockeyed for a look through one of the huge portholes outside the pilots' mess. The once black and distant mass of the pulsar now took over the view, its edges streaked by dying stars. The pulsar reminded Maniac of Scylla, though it flashed brilliantly every three seconds. The other pilots took no pleasure in the carrier's present position. Maniac would educate them. He drew back from the porthole and addressed his audience. "Do you know what you people are staring at? Do you have any idea?"

With a sigh, Hunter replied, "A Class Two pulsar, mate. I've seen a lot of 'em."

"No." He cocked his thumb toward the porthole. "That, ladies and gentlemen, is the ultimate rush."

Sure, the others looked at him as though he were crazy. He could live with that.

As long as he had Forbes smiling.

Which he did.

Blair took up a position near the back of the bridge, beside Deveraux. She noticed him and edged away. He gave a slight snort and held his ground.

A triangle of consoles divided the forward bridge, with the helmsman seated at the triangle's top and gripping his wheel. Sansky and Gerald manned observation consoles at the bottom angles. Taggart stood at the helmsman's shoulder, having carefully chosen his position.

Sansky touched a key on the shipwide intercom panel. "Ladies and gentlemen, this is the captain. I'll put an end to the rumors by informing you that in sixty seconds we're going to jump the Class Two pulsar directly ahead. We've been ordered to the Ulysses Corridor, and we need to get there quickly." Sansky went on to give a capsule summary of the events surrounding the destruction of the Pegasus Station. When he finished, he looked over his shoulder at everyone on the bridge, and Blair found his own fear mirrored in the captain's face. "May God be with us all." Then Sansky favored the helmsman with a nod. "Take us in."

The carrier lurched a moment, then started for the pulsar. Anything that wasn't battened down—and even a few things that were—began to tremble with a sound that reminded Blair of the earthquakes on Nephele. He found a nearby railing and gripped it for support. Deveraux folded her arms over her chest, refusing to join him.

As they glided closer to the pulsar, it better resembled Scylla, but this Scylla, maybe a distant cousin, had only one head and the twinkling eye of a Cyclops. She gobbled up stars, planets, planetoids, and smaller debris. In her work Blair sensed a perfect balance, a simplicity that tingled at the base of his spine.

He felt her magnetic fields.

And in his mind's eye, he saw an avenue through space-time itself, a shiny black funnel of infinite mass that he sensed promised infinite awareness.

"Attention! Attention! Course error. Adjust course immediately," came the NAVCOM's automated voice. An alarm squawked.

"Ignore that," Taggart said. "Helm. Hold steady as she goes."

"Captain," the NAVCOM called out. "The ship is headed into the Point of No Return zone of an uncharted Class Two pulsar. One minute before gravitational pull is one hundred percent."

Sansky spun toward the helm. "What about it, Taggart?"

"The readings are wrong. Your AI's sensors are not calibrated to the pulsar. They've already been warped by the gravitational field."

"I must insist that we change course immediately," the NAVCOM argued. "Initiating AI override."

"No!" Taggart screamed.

The *Tiger Claw* suddenly bucked, and Deveraux came crashing forward into the railing, near Blair. She found her grip as the ship began pulling to port, throwing them parallel to the rail.

Taggart, who now held fast to the helmsman's console, shouldered his way to a touchpad. "Manual override! Now! Disregard your artificial intelligence—or we're all dead."

"Captain," Gerald said through clenched teeth. "I believe you should reconsider."

Sansky cocked a brow. "I already have. Steady as she goes, helm."

Like a cosmic predator with claws of gravitational force, the pulsar reached out and grabbed the carrier. Fighting to stabilize the ship's pitch and yaw, the helmsman ground his teeth as the carrier's bulkheads shook and her ceiling threatened to cave in.

"This is the captain," Sansky said over the intercom. "Brace for jump point interphase. Fifteen seconds to jump point."

But Blair scarcely heard the captain, scarcely saw the bridge or felt the rail. His senses began shutting down as they had when nearing Scylla.

And the feeling, the awe-inspiring feeling, lived in him. He saw the entire Ulysses Corridor as effortlessly as he saw his own hand. He saw Nephele, the Sol system, whatever he wanted to see, because distances no longer held meaning. Time no longer held meaning. He thought of his mother. And there, before him, she gave a mild frown, her hair and complexion as smooth and dark as he remembered. "You shouldn't do this to yourself, Christopher. You weren't meant to see me. This is not your continuum."

"It is mine. I chose it."

"You don't have the right to choose. Only one does."

"What do you mean? There aren't any rules. I feel this. I can do what I feel."

"Then you'll fall. Like the others."

"You're not my mother, are you?"

"I'm everything your mother was, is, and will be. I'm in every part of the universe at once, as you are now, as you shouldn't be."

"Why?"

"I wish you could understand. I wish that more than anything. But I've seen your path. And there's nothing I can do to change it." Her features grew younger, more narrow, until Blair stared at Lieutenant Commander Deveraux, who said, "Didn't you hear him, Lieutenant? Fifteen seconds to jump. Better hang on."

He reached with trembling hands for the rail and blinked as a burst of light shot from the pulsar.

Then he found Taggart staring at him. Blair could only imagine

Top: Todd "Maniac"
Marshall (Matt Lillard),
Christopher Blair
(Freddie Prinze, Jr.) and
James Taggart aka
Paladin (Tcheky Karyo).

Right: Jeannette
"Angel" Devereaux
(Saffron Burrows)

(Top) The Kilrathi attack on the Command
Center at Vega Sector Fleet Headquarters.

(Bottom) Confederation Broadsword
bomber attacking a Kilrathi Dreadnought

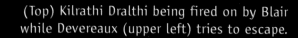

(Top) Kilrathi Dralthi being fired on by Blair while Devereaux (upper left) tries to escape.

(Bottom) Captain Sansky (David Suchet) on the deck of the *Tiger Claw*.

(Above) A Kilrathi pilot.

(Right) Blair in a Marine combat suit entering Kilrathi ship.

(Opposite page, Top) Confederation Marines on board the *Tiger Claw*.

(Opposite page, Bottom) Kilrathi general (with beard) facing Kilrathi soldier.

(Left) Maniac being "questioned" by Devereaux.

(Bottom) Rapier plane under attack on the flight deck of the *Tiger Claw*.

(Opposite page, Top) Kilrathi soldiers on the attack.

(Opposite page, Bottom) Kilrathi Cruiser (on left) attacking the *Tiger Claw*.

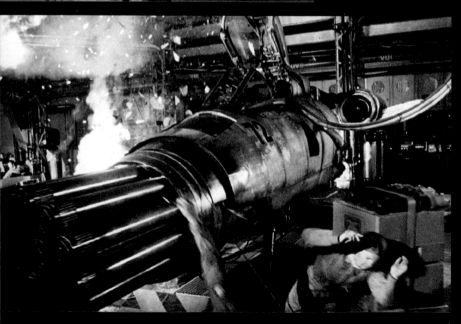

Confederation missiles destroying Kilrathi Destroyer; Kilrathi Dreadnought in the rear.

how strange he looked. He had not just seen a ghost.

He had seen the universe itself.

And the experience had left him frightened of who he was and might become.

No warning had stunned him more.

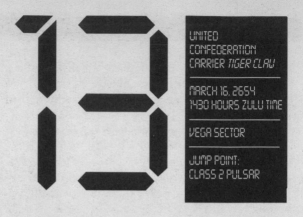

13

UNITED
CONFEDERATION
CARRIER *TIGER CLAW*

MARCH 16, 2654
1430 HOURS ZULU TIME

VEGA SECTOR

JUMP POINT:
CLASS 2 PULSAR

Blair clung to the bridge's railing. The vibrations increased, and he nearly slipped to the floor. Deveraux, too, struggled to keep standing, her poker face failing as the pulsar tightened its grip.

Taggart kept his cool and held tight to the helmsman's chair, alternating his gaze between screens and viewports. "Steady now. Steady . . ."

Apparently bored with simply tugging on the carrier, the pulsar decided to jerk the *Tiger Claw* in as though she were a sailfish on a line. The force sent Deveraux crashing into Blair. They fell away from the railing and rose to grab the bulkhead.

"What was that?" Deveraux asked.

"The ship's trying to tear itself free of the space-time fabric," Blair said, his stomach acting out a similar battle.

Growing in pitch, the vibrations continued until Blair's ears filled with a single, deafening hum. The pulsar flashed again, momentarily blinding him. As his vision cleared, he looked down to see Deveraux's hand reaching toward his shoulder—

And at that moment, the *Tiger Claw* plunged into the pulsar, into the gap in the space-time continuum calculated by Taggart.

The hum, the vibrations, and the taste of bile at the back of

Blair's throat all fell off into nothingness. He should feel more comfortable in the moment, knowing what to expect. But the feeling had returned, and it sang a bewitching song, trying to lure him out to explore the universe.

Then you'll fall. Like the others.

Such power. And only a thought away. How could he control it? How could anyone control it? The only thing that kept him in place was the fear caused by his mother. Even with a perfect sense of direction and the power to experience the universe in a single breath, he would still struggle to find happiness, love, friendship, hope, wisdom, all of the things that defined being human.

Or he could choose to abandon them.

Christopher Blair stood at a cosmic crossroads, and he refused to make a decision, refused to surrender to the powerful feeling. If he did that, he felt it would forever control him.

He searched his thoughts for a way to live with the feeling, but a powerful shudder pulled him away. His senses returned with an electrifying vengeance. He gagged as the harsh roar of the carrier's passage echoed through the bridge. Sansky, Gerald, Taggart, and the helmsman, once statues, now fought to maintain balance.

Deveraux's hand finally settled on Blair's shoulder, and as he turned to look at her, the deck buckled and tossed her into him. They fell back toward the bulkhead, and Deveraux's forehead struck the durasteel with a thud that made Blair flinch. She dropped to her knees, and he grabbed her shoulders, shifting her back. He tilted her chin up to observe a bleeding cut on her forehead. "Are you all right?"

Her eyes seemed vague, her head swaying. "We make it?"

A glance to the bank of forward viewports gave Blair his reply. The pulsar had slid back into her gloomy cavern of gravity that lay four days and three jump points away. In the distance appeared a massive planet, a gas giant banded in yellow and orange. Several large spots blemished its surface, and tiny points of light hovered about it, moons gliding peacefully in their orbits. Beyond the Jovian-like system lay the darkness of space. "We're through the jump point."

Even as Blair finished telling her, the carrier's alarms clicked off, and the rumbling deck and bulkheads grew still.

Taggart considered the helmsman's screen, then glanced through the viewport. "Ladies and gentlemen, welcome to the Ulysses Corridor."

Lieutenant Commander Obutu craned his head toward Captain Sansky, one hand on his headset. "Launching Rapiers. Now."

After a few seconds, two fighters shot by the viewport, their afterburners aglow. Blair followed their path until they climbed out of view.

"Shields up," Sansky ordered, getting to his feet. "Mr. Obutu, stealth mode, please."

Obutu threw a toggle. Every console grew dim, and standard lighting darkened to red. "Going to stealth. Seven percent electronic emissions, zero communications."

Arriving at the radar station, Sansky leaned over the beanpole of a boy seated there. "Status?"

"Scanners picking up strong electromagnetic signature at one-eleven mark four-three. An asteroid field. I'd say she's a Kilrathi, sir."

Sansky nodded, then brought himself to full height to consult with an angry-looking Gerald.

Meanwhile, Blair struggled to his feet. "Don't move," he told Deveraux. "I'll be right back." He hustled to the rear of the bridge and unclipped a first aid kit from the wall. He returned with the kit and removed a laser pen from its holder. "Don't move," he said, then lifted the pen to her forehead.

"You already said that."

"This time I really mean it." He thumbed on the power and began sealing the cut. "You're a good patient," he said softly, then his aim shifted.

"Ouch."

"Sorry." He finished the seal, lowered the pen, and edged closer to her, studying his work.

"It's all right," she assured him, drawing back. She lifted her brow, breaking the seal.

He quickly shook his head and brought the laser pen toward her. "It's still bleeding. If I—"

"It's all right," she insisted, then grabbed his wrist, forcing the pen away.

"Yes, ma'am." He stood and proffered his hand.

She dismissed the offer. Using the bulkhead for support, she clambered to her feet.

Blair opened his mouth, wanting to tell her he was sorry, that all he had wanted to do was help. He also wanted to say that her perfume made him lightheaded, that her skin seemed like the smooth surface of some ripe, exotic fruit, and that he would like to explore the secrets in her hair. He wanted to tell her most of that, well, some of that, but Captain Sansky suddenly came between them. "That head all right?" he asked Deveraux.

"Little scratch. I'm fine."

"Good. Security patrol's been launched, but I'm keeping them in tight. I want you to prepare a recon. I want to know what's out there."

"Yes, sir." She started for the corridor.

"And Deveraux," Sansky called after her. "No contact with the enemy. Not yet."

She looked over her shoulder and nodded, then faced Blair. "Let's go, Lieutenant."

As they left the bridge, Captain Sansky spoke on the intercom: "As most of you have guessed, we just made one heck of a jump. It is now oh-three-hundred hours, March seventeeth, and we've taken a shortcut into the Ulysses Corridor, where, as I told you, the Pegasus Station was attacked and destroyed. The main Kilrathi battle group is in the quadrant and headed for the Charybdis Quasar. In just over ten hours it'll be in position to jump into Earth space. Our mission is to find the Kilrathi, assess their capacities and plan of action, and if necessary, stop them. We're the only Confed ship in the area, people. We'll have no help and no rescue. We can only count on each other. That is all."

The stars, once tiny points of light, had shifted into a swirl of glistening claw marks. Admiral Geoffrey Tolwyn sat at an observation console, thinking about those marks and what lay beyond them. He imagined the future, imagined his battle group arriving in Earth space two hours too late. The once-blue planet would be dark. Kilrathi bio-missiles would be exploding in her atmosphere and whipping up thick clouds of poison gas that would descend upon her citizens for several months, killing the millions who couldn't make it to shelters and destroying all plants and animals. It would take a thousand years or more for the planet to recover. Tolwyn beat a fist on the console. Two hours. One hundred and twenty minutes.

Someone approached from behind, and Tolwyn considered turning around, but he recognized the light footsteps. "What is it, Commodore?"

"Message from Earth Command, sir. Their defenses are online, but—"

"They don't believe they can withstand a Kilrathi battle group without fleet support."

"No, sir. But they will fight. Earth will never surrender."

"Surrender? That's not an option with the Kilrathi. They believe they're the supreme race. The rest of us are just here to do one thing."

"What's that?"

Tolwyn snickered. "To die." He swiveled his chair to take in Bellegarde's serious face. "Our status?"

"We're still running at one hundred and ten percent. But we've already lost three ships, two at jump points, one from a reactor meltdown."

"Run at one-twenty."

"We'll lose more of the battle group."

"One-twenty, Commodore."

"One-twenty. Aye-aye, sir."

Blair changed into his flight suit, then headed down to the flight deck. He found Deveraux standing near the lift doors, waiting for him. She gave a quick nod and turned toward the Rapiers. Blair crossed in front of her to check her wound.

"Would you cut that out?" she said.

"Sorry. I think it'll heal okay. I don't want you to have a scar."

"Too late. I've cornered the market on those. C'mon."

They walked down the flight line, past a row of Broadsword bombers. Techs stood atop, below, or beside the bombers, some in the blue glow of torches, some on rolling ladders. Fumes from fuel and heated metal filled the air.

"Any standard operating procedure I should know about?" Blair asked as they neared the first line of Rapiers.

"No SOP out here," Deveraux said. "There's only one rule."

"Don't get killed?"

"Don't get *me* killed." She broke off toward one of two fully armed Rapiers, their short wings slightly bowing under the weight of Dumb-fire, Spiculum IR, and Pilum Friend or Foe missiles locked to over- or under-wing hardpoints.

Blair followed her, taking a closer look at her fighter. He noted her call sign: "Angel." Then he saw the many rows of kill marks. He counted them. "Twenty-six. Wow."

"That puts me ahead of the law of averages," she said, mounting her cockpit ladder. "Well ahead. The curve'll catch up to me sooner or later." She tipped her head toward the Rapier next to hers. "Your bird, Blair. Treat her well."

Only then did Blair recognize the Rapier's number: thirty-five. They had given him Bossman's old fighter. Chen's name had been removed, along with his kill marks. The yellow paint used to stencil LT. CHRISTOPHER BLAIR below the cockpit seemed too new, too perfect against the Rapier's battered armor.

Although he had never known Vince Chen, he felt a tinge of guilt over taking the man's fighter, as though he were spoiling Chen's memory. But he shouldn't feel that way. Taking the fighter out again would be in tribute to Bossman's life, to what he held most dear. If Chen were like most pilots, he would want it that way.

Blair gently touched the mighty nose cannon. "She's all mine," he told Deveraux, beaming.

"And she'll probably be someone else's. Mount up. The clock is ticking."

"One more question. Why me for this recon?"

"Why not?"

"Yeah," he said, only half-buying her reply. "Why not." He jogged up the ladder and lowered himself into the pit.

Once tight in his harness, he ran through the preflight check. Meanwhile, ground crews below made their final walkarounds of both fighters, running scanners and their own gazes over every seal and double-checking the weapons. Blair threw a pair of toggles, powering up the thrusters as Deveraux did the same. The engines purred and made Blair feel as though he were flexing his muscles. He slipped on his headset, helmet, and O_2 mask, then dialed up Deveraux's comm channel. "Maverick to Angel. Comm check. Roger."

"Comm established," she replied, flashing him a thumbs-up on the left VDU. "Lieutenant, your call sign is Maverick? Where'd you get that? From some old movie?"

"Actually, ma'am, it's been a standing joke for a while now. Back at the academy, I had a rep for being a by-the-book flyer. So, of course, they called me Maverick. And yeah, I did see that old movie. They flew those big heavy atmospheric fighters. Must've been fun back then."

"We'll never know. All moorings are clear. External power disengaged. Internal systems nominal, roger."

"Roger. I'm fully detached and ninety-five into the sequence," Blair said, reading his panels.

The deckmaster waved Deveraux toward her launch position. Her Rapier rose several meters, then floated forward as the landing skids folded into the fighter's belly. She lined up with the runway and the shining energy field beyond.

"Lieutenant Commander, you are cleared to launch," Blair heard the flight boss tell Deveraux.

"Roger, Boss. See you on the flip." She punctuated her sentence with a blast of thrusters that cast Blair's Rapier in a tawny sheen. Like a finned bullet, she blew out of the hangar.

"All right, Lieutenant. Let's see if you remember how to do this," the flight boss said tiredly.

Without a word, Blair took his Rapier into a hover and, following the deckmaster's signals, lined up for launch. He would perform a textbook takeoff that would shut the boss's mouth.

"That looks good, young man," the boss said, as though inspecting Blair's coloring book. "You're all clear."

Throttling up to exactly eighty percent thruster power (the textbook's suggestion), Blair tore off toward the energy field, bulkheads whirring by, the stars clouded by what looked like a wall of water. The Rapier shimmied as he passed through the field and burst into open space. He climbed away from the *Tiger Claw*, accelerating to full throttle, then flicked his gaze to the radar display, finding the blue blip of Deveraux's fighter. He banked sharply to form on her wing. With his free hand, he unzipped his flight suit, dug out his Pilgrim cross, and gave it a squeeze for luck. A signal from Deveraux lit up his right display: KEEP RADIO SILENCE.

Ahead lay a small, rocky world, covered in shadow and orbiting a distant and dimly burning brown dwarf star. Blair targeted the planet, and data spilled across his right display. Officially catalogued as Planetoid SX34B5, it looked very similar to Earth's moon. Blair targeted the brown dwarf and quickly scanned the information on the star's size, age, and something about it not having enough mass to convert hydrogen into helium by way of nuclear fusion. He stopped reading when the data became too technical but still felt satisfied with his inspection. Some pilots like Maniac flew into the unknown relying only on their eyes. Blair had been taught that a physical understanding of his combat environment would allow him to use it as an ally, not an obstacle.

He switched his targeting cross-hairs to a field of asteroids encircling the brown dwarf. Jagged chunks of ice-covered rock tumbled slowly and occasionally collided with others, breaking into smaller pieces.

Deveraux's Rapier jumped a little ahead of his, and Blair noted the cue. They would move into and sweep the field. He slid over the Heads Up Display viewer on his helmet, then, with one eye, studied the digitized tactical schematic. Dozens of reticles singled out targets, outlined them, and flashed, then sensors gave him an instant report of their position. Green lines formed into a glide path through the thousands of spinning rocks.

But not all of the debris appeared natural. Shiny objects began peeking out from behind the rocks, objects that became more distinct—pieces of durasteel shredded like paper.

A particularly huge plate, twisted and scorched, spun by his canopy. He recoiled a little as he spotted the letters ASUS painted near its edge.

"Angel? Did you catch that? That's from Pegasus."

She appeared on his left display. "You just broke radio silence, Lieutenant."

"I'm sorry. I just—"

"Forget it." She shook her head, then looked up, taking in more of the asteroid field. "Concussion must've blown pieces of the station all over the sector." Her tactical computer chirped.

Blair's computer answered with a chirp of its own. A blip flashed across his radar, then another, then both disappeared. "I just picked up multiple contacts, bearing—"

"Pipe down. I'm getting something . . ."

And Blair spotted them, too: six blips burning brightly in his radar, headed directly for their position.

"Angel—"

"Radio silence. And let's get deeper into this field. Low power. We'll see if we can wait 'em out."

"Roger."

She dove ahead, following the digitized glide path through the asteroids. Blair kept tight on her six o'clock until she veered sixty degrees to port and settled in the lee of an oblong-shaped rock nearly one hundred meters long. Blair raced by her, finding cover of his own below a similar rock about five hundred meters away. He frantically switched off everything except for life support and sat there a moment, the oxygen whistling softly into his mask, the sweat beading on his brow. His gaze traced the thick veins of ice that fanned out across the stone. He tried to concentrate on something as boring as the rock, but the suspense had his skin crawling.

"My scanners are blind, Merlin. Talk to me."

The little man knew better than to appear in Blair's cockpit, perhaps creating a detectable energy source. Instead, he transferred himself into the Rapier's main computer, where he could speak without his holographic form. A dim light flashed in the right display as he replied, "Crosstalk between a large Kilrathi vessel and the brown dwarf down there. I can't decipher the code."

"They know we're here?"

"Possibly. From the sophistication of the equipment on board, I'd say the vessel is a Command and Communications module."

"So what's it commanding?"

"At least six other ships near the brown dwarf are communicating with it. Interesting. I'm picking up an Ultra Low Frequency signal. The Rapier's scanners aren't equipped to receive or detect ULF."

"What's it mean? This frequency?"

"It's a primitive pulse technology, Ultra Low Frequency. Very slow, but it carries over extreme distances, not unlike tom-toms. Pilgrims used ULF during the war."

"So why would the Kilrathi—" Blair caught himself. "Did you say *Pilgrims*?"

"Yes. I believe I did."

"Then you know more about the Pilgrims? You told me my father wiped your flash memory."

"I . . . I don't know how I know about the ULF signals," Merlin stammered. "I just do. Perhaps that data is buried in my suboperating memory, left over from the war. Maybe it's intuition."

"Intuition?" Blair fought off a chill. He could deal with Merlin's sarcasm. But a PPC with intuition? "Well, do you have signal source?"

"It appears to be coming from quadrant thirty."

"That puts it near the *Tiger Claw*. Can you translate it?"

"The code isn't in my . . ." Merlin broke off.

"What?"

"They're scanning the rocks."

"Merlin off."

Emerald light flickered above, and Blair could almost feel the scanning beam as it passed over the rock.

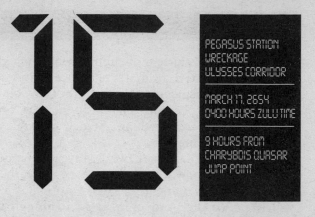

15

PEGASUS STATION
WRECKAGE
ULYSSES CORRIDOR

MARCH 17, 2654
0400 HOURS ZULU TIME

9 HOURS FROM
CHARYBDIS QUASAR
JUMP POINT

"Go on," Deveraux whispered to herself. "There's nothing in this mouse hole. Beat it."

The Kilrathi ship continued probing, its beam throwing a green halo over the asteroid.

A thump from the port side caught her attention.

She shuddered as a figure dressed in Confederation Marine Corps armor floated near her wing. She looked away before the face rolled into view, but her stomach dropped anyway—and not from nausea. The Rapier had begun drifting.

Unable to fire retros that would reveal her location, she watched as the starboard wing brushed against an uneven valley of ice and rock with a sickening creak. She shushed her fighter and looked up. "You didn't read that," she told the Kilrathi. "And if you did, it was just two rocks colliding."

She waited. Waited some more. Became an authority on waiting. Knew the details. The frustration. Could tell you all you wanted to know about it. Could tell you that in the end there was, of course, nothing to do but wait.

And react.

The asteroid's halo grew brighter.

◆　　　◆　　　◆

Far to port, past clusters of rubble, something glimmered. Was it just more durasteel from the Pegasus Station? A second look proved Blair's suspicions. The Kilrathi ConCom ship had paused near Deveraux's position. "What do they see, Merlin?"

"They don't *see* anything. Switch on your thermal scanner. They're out of range to detect it."

He slid the HUD viewer over his eye and tapped on the scanner. Not much of a view: the glimmer once more, the asteroids among twinkling shards of metal . . .

There. A fading red glow shown through the massive rock shielding Deveraux. "They've spotted Angel's heat corona."

"Two more Kilrathi closing fast," Merlin said anxiously. "Probably fighters."

Blair's gloved fingers traveled quickly over his instrument panels. Displays rose from darkness. Scanners flashed data to him. Engines hummed in their warming sequence. The communications system gave a readiness beep. "Angel. They've spotted us. Two more bogies coming in hot. Six o'clock." He stole a glance at his radar display. No, the Kilrathi weren't changing their minds.

Deveraux's wide eyes filled his display. "Can't spot them, Blair. Call it."

The blips moved closer.

"Jack in the box," Blair instructed. "On three. One . . . two . . ."

The Rapier's engines ignited with a thundering roar. Jagged stone wiped past him as he skimmed along the asteroid's surface. Once clear of the rock, he corkscrewed straight up, out of the field and into a starry sky.

"Form on my wing," Deveraux ordered.

"Yes, ma'am!" Wheeling around, Blair rocketed toward her fighter, strangling more thrust from his Rapier. As he neared her position, he spotted two Dralthi fighters escorting the ConCom ship.

Without giving the enemy pilots time to blink, he and Deveraux squeezed off dumb-fire missiles. Her rocket tore past the left Dralthi's shields to swallow the fighter in a fireball. His missile caught the other Dralthi as it began veering off. The explosion tore away the ship's engine housing and sent it spiraling out of control. It glanced several times off the asteroid Deveraux had used for cover, shedding plastisteel like a cybernetic snake.

Charging through the still-lingering blast waves, he and Deveraux targeted the ConCom ship. Even as his sensors indicated that she had ignited her missile, Blair jammed down his trigger. Their projectiles trailed ribbons of exhaust as they traveled the thousand-meter gap. But they stopped short, detonating in useless ringlets of energy as the ConCom's powerful shields absorbed them.

"Well, they're awake now," Blair said. He checked his radar display. "I've got two more bogies coming up from the brown dwarf. Engaging."

"Negative! I count fourteen unfriendlies inbound. Looks like two destroyers. We are out of here!" Her exhaust ports flared as afterburners engaged.

Blair lit his own burners and banked suddenly, following her back toward the *Tiger Claw*. He switched his left VDU to the rear turret display. A swarm of glowing specs descended upon the asteroid field.

Standing in the center of the *Grist'Ar'roc*'s bridge, Captain Thiraka nar Kiranka thought about the report from his tactical officer. Then he moved cautiously toward the rear of the bridge, where Kalralahr Bokoth crouched on bent knee below a meter-high statue of Sivar. Waiting at the proper distance, Thiraka hoped the admiral would notice him soon.

As though emerging dizzy from a vision, the admiral craned his pale, oblong head toward Thiraka. "Kal Shintahr?"

"Sir, our lead ConCom ship has engaged a Confederation reconnaissance flight in sector seven. Fighters from two of our destroyers were dispatched to intercept."

"And the reconnaissance patrol escaped." With a slight growl, Bokoth forced himself to his feet. "So the *Tiger Claw* is here."

"Yes. The merchantman we tracked earlier jumped into this sector by using a gravity well. And the carrier jumped here through a pulsar."

"Do we have a fix on her signal?"

"We do."

The admiral turned to the command chair, where, cloaked in shadows and nutrient haze, a figure stirred. "Your friend is dedicated," Bokoth said, his words translated into the hoots and squeaks made by humans.

Stepping forward, the hairless ape in the atmospheric suit raised one of its stubby fingers and replied, "My friend is a Pilgrim. This is what he trained for. Prepare the ambush."

"In time," Bokoth said, raising his paw.

"That ship is the only thing that stands between us and the success of this mission. It's yours for the taking."

Bokoth absently tugged on his whiskers, purring into a thought. "That ship is insignificant. That hate of your kind blinds you. All things pass. Let it go."

The ape took a step closer. "You're wrong. Most things pass: love, passion, anger, life. One is eternal: hate."

"We read your After Action Report," Commander Gerald said, staring angrily at Blair as he and Deveraux stood on the *Tiger Claw*'s bridge. "You knew what the orders were. No contact with the enemy. Now you've compromised the mission and this ship."

"Sir. I had no choice. The enemy had spotted Lieutenant Commander Deveraux's heat signature, sir."

"Really," Gerald said, half-singing the word. His gaze shifted radically. "Angel, how sure are you that the Kilrathi had you targeted? Given the lieutenant's background . . ."

"Excuse me?" Blair's face grew hot.

"It's well documented that Pilgrim saboteurs have been responsible for much of the Confed's problems in this war. I'll be sure to download that information to your account, Lieutenant."

"Did they have me targeted?" Deveraux demanded, turning to face Blair. "Or did you just get trigger-happy?"

"Trigger-happy? What kind of an operator do you—"

"Enough," Sansky said. "The Kilrathi are aware that Rapiers are short-range fighting craft assigned to cap ships. They know we're close by." He focused on Blair. "Tell me again about this communication you claim to have heard."

"It was a ULF signal coming from the vicinity of the *Tiger Claw*, sir."

Sansky swung toward the navigation station. "What about it, NAVCOM? Were any communications sent from this ship?"

"Negative, Captain," the computer said. "There were no communications sent by the *Tiger Claw*."

Gerald smirked and gave a nod.

"Sir, I tell you—"

"You tell me nothing, Lieutenant," Sansky said. "Nor does your flight recorder. A Rapier's scanners are not equipped to detect ULF transmissions. Your reliance on your PPC—unauthorized equipment, I might add—does not convince me that the signal exists. PPCs are not standard military issue and are vulnerable to a number of viruses. What you thought you heard—"

"But sir—"

"—could've come from any number of natural sources."

"This was not a natural—"

"Dismissed, Lieutenant."

Captain Sansky took a moment to recover from his argument with the young lieutenant. He admired Blair's courage to hold his ground, even on the bridge. He turned to Gerald. "Your assessment?"

"That ConCom's running point for the battle group. Their fleet won't be far behind. As you said, they know we're here, so I say we send them a message. I can have my fighters up in thirty minutes."

"Twenty," Deveraux corrected, her self-confidence revving even higher than Gerald's.

"That would be a mistake," Taggart said, lifting his head from the helmsman's screen. "Without her fighters, this ship's vulnerable."

Pursing his lips, Sansky thought about the pros and cons of a first strike.

"You're a civilian scout," Gerald reminded Taggart, "not a naval officer. Tactical operations are our concern."

Taggart's face grew rigid, and his tone plunged to warning

depths. "There's a great deal more at stake here than you seem to understand, Commander."

Sansky threw up a hand. "The XO is right. I'm sorry, Mr. Taggart. Destroying that ConCom and its escorts will slow the Kilrathi. Deveraux will lead a strike force. You will accompany her." He crossed back to Lieutenant Commander Obutu, who kept vigil over his screens. "Con, plot a course for the rings of Planet Four-fifteen. We'll find good cover there."

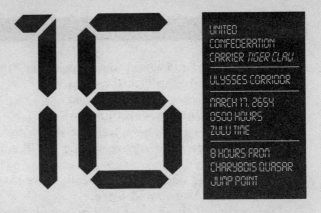

16

UNITED
CONFEDERATION
CARRIER *TIGER CLAW*

ULYSSES CORRIDOR

MARCH 17, 2654
0500 HOURS
ZULU TIME

8 HOURS FROM
CHARYBDIS QUASAR
JUMP POINT

When Deveraux had left the bridge with orders to lead a strike force to take out the Kilrathi ConCom ship, she had headed directly to her quarters to shower, change into a clean flight suit, and sit at her desk to meditate.

Now she opened her eyes, reached across her desk, and switched on the holovid player.

A small girl seated on the edge of a picnic blanket glimmered at the foot of her bunk. A young man rolled a pink ball toward the girl, while a young woman looked on with a proud grin.

Her hatch bell rang and startled her. She stood, paused the holovid, then moved to the door. Not many people came to see Deveraux because everyone knew how she liked her privacy during stand-down. She touched the open key.

And lost a heartbeat.

"I need to talk to you." Blair leaned on the doorjamb, his face long, his eyes reflective pools.

She forgot to breathe. She glanced to the holovid, the figures unmoving—

Blair pushed his way past her.

"Hey. You can't barge into my—"

He spun around and tossed something to her. "I wear it for luck."
She caught then examined the cross.

"It was my mother's," he explained.

"Is your luck at odds with our mission?"

That drew a long sigh from him. He shifted away, surveying the rest of her quarters, his gaze falling on the paused holovid. "What's this?"

"Nothing," she said, then practically dove toward the holovid and shut it off. "You should leave."

"You worried about gossip? I'm not. I already know what they're saying about me."

"You give them reason to talk."

He searched the ceiling for a reply, then finally said, "You think he's right about me?"

"Who? Gerald?"

"Yeah. I mean, in his mind I started selling out the *Tiger Claw* the moment I stepped on board."

Her gaze flicked to the cross. "I don't see how you can be a Pilgrim and fight on our side."

"I'm not a Pilgrim. I don't even know what a Pilgrim is."

"You're not that naïve—otherwise you'd keep this thing in a box."

"I guess you're right. My mother was an off-worlder who grew up hating Earth, hating humanity. My father fought for the Confederation. Somehow, despite all the hate, they found each other."

"How?"

"I don't know. They died before I was five. He was killed trying to save her in the Peron Massacre. That cross is all I have. I'm not sure where I belong, Commander, except here, fighting and flying."

As she turned the cross over in her hands, Deveraux felt a chill spidering across her neck. "Sit down, Lieutenant."

He moved toward her bunk, but she directed him to the chair at her desk.

"Why do you think they call me Angel?" she asked.

His shoulders lifted in a half-shrug.

"It's a real weeper. Headlines: My parents died in the same war. I grew up in an orphanage on Earth, in Brussels."

Their gazes met, and Deveraux sensed an even stronger connection.

"At night, I'd cry for them," she continued. "The sisters told me they were angels. I kept crying for them to come and take me to heaven. But they weren't angels. They were dead. Gone. It was like they had never existed."

"Like Bossman?"

Deveraux held herself for a moment, forcing her breath to steady, her hands to stop trembling. "Emotion gets in the way of our mission. There is no emotion. Only the job. You sight the target, terminate it, and move on without looking back."

"Commander, emotion is what separates us from the Pilgrims. And the Kilrathi."

She leaned back on the bulkhead and felt the sting of tears. "Lieutenant Commander Chen was . . . Bossman and I got close. Too close. And then he got himself killed."

Blair rose, reaching out to comfort her.

She motioned him off, then backhanded the tears away. "Consider what you just saw classified."

He lowered his hand and smiled just enough to make her feel better. "Yes, ma'am. And can I ask you something?"

"That depends."

"You said that your parents were killed in the same war. Were they killed by Pilgrims?"

Her gaze searched his. "You want to know what side my family was on, is that it, Lieutenant?"

"Actually, I was wondering more about you." He looked at the cross.

"I don't know how they were killed."

"Wouldn't you like to know?"

"I've already tried to find out. Those records were lost."

He looked to the holovid player. "Is that your cross?"

"Lieutenant, we're square. You saved me today. And I have a few things to finish here." She handed him the cross.

With a curt nod, he headed for the hatch.

"And Blair," she called after him. "Gerald's a clown."

His eyes thanked her.

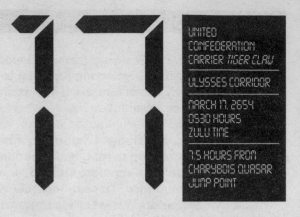

11

UNITED
CONFEDERATION
CARRIER *TIGER CLAW*

ULYSSES CORRIDOR

MARCH 17, 2654
0530 HOURS
ZULU TIME

7.5 HOURS FROM
CHARYBDIS QUASAR
JUMP POINT

Blair finished a walkaround inspection of his Rapier, then joined the other pilots milling about the flight line, waiting for Lieutenant Commander Deveraux.

The nearby lift doors opened, exposing Maniac and Forbes, both still pulling on their uniforms. They hustled out of the lift to the laughter of their comrades—all except Blair.

"Targets locked," Blair muttered, then set his jaw and walked toward Maniac. "Did you change the lock code?"

"What are you talking about?"

"The lock code on our hatch? I couldn't get in." He scowled at Forbes. "And I heard laughing from inside, but no one would answer."

Maniac slapped a paw on his shoulder. "Someday, Blair, you're gonna look back and say, 'God, I wish I'd been him.'"

"Someday, I'm going to look back and—"

"Ten-hut!" Knight shouted.

Blair abandoned his reply and scrambled to the line with the other jocks. They assumed the pose as Lieutenant Commander Deveraux walked down the row, her face unreadable. "All right, ladies, listen up. We have a ConCom with escorts. That means two, possibly three Ralari-class destroyers with their fighters and support ships. Primary target is the ConCom. Everything else is gravy." She paused before Blair. "Let's make 'em bleed. Mount up!"

As Blair headed to his fighter, he passed Hunter, who, as usual, champed his cigar and brushed that long hair out of his face. Blair thought of wishing the man luck, but as he looked up, he saw how Hunter made a point of ignoring him, so he went straight for his cockpit ladder.

"Blair," Deveraux called out. "Take Hunter's wing."

"I got his wing, ma'am."

Failing to remove his cigar, Hunter said, "Ma'am, I'd just as soon you assign me another wingman."

Deveraux came toward Hunter, who had mistakenly lit the fire in her eyes. "You have some problem I should be aware of, Hunter?"

The big Australian sneered at Blair. "Yes, ma'am, I do. I don't fly with Pilgrims."

"Then maybe you don't fly at all."

"Ma'am, I think you want me for this op."

With disgust all but dripping from her face, Deveraux thought a second, then said, "Blair. You'll fly *my* wing."

"Are you sure about that?" he asked.

Her eyes snapped wide. "Did I just give you a suggestion or an order?"

"I got your wing, ma'am."

She tossed an ugly look in Hunter's direction, then left.

"Hey," Hunter said.

Blair hesitated.

"You put me or my shipmates in danger, half-breed, I'll kill you."

"You'll try." He stared hard at the man, then pounded up his ladder. "It's all one big lovefest," he moaned.

The launch went off without a hitch, save for Polanski's report of a hydraulic leak too insignificant to ground him.

Blair held a steady course at Deveraux's four o'clock low. They, along with the other Rapier pilots, escorted two Broadswords piloted by Taggart and Knight. Originally designed as an attack bomber for Kilrathi capital ships, the Broadsword held its own as an all-purpose fighter, equipped with port, starboard, and aft turrets as well as four missile and four torpedo hardpoints. If a Broadsword got close enough to a capital ship (or in their present situation, a Kilrathi ConCom ship), its torpedoes would successfully penetrate phase shields. Thus, getting Taggart and Knight in close enough to the ConCom ship remained the first objective. Accomplishing that meant punching a hole through the enemy fighters surely waiting for them.

They came up fast on the ring of asteroids and debris orbiting the brown dwarf. Blair slid his HUD viewer into place and surveyed the zone with thermal scanners, finding it cool and clear. The strike force wove into the field, huge rocks and splintered durasteel tumbling by, some pieces just meters away.

Suddenly Maniac's masked face and big, round eyes lit up Blair's display. "All right, losers, listen up. I got three confirmed targets at five o'clock, bugging the brown dwarf."

"Confirm that," Forbes said. "Middle one has a massive electromagnetic signature."

"It's the ConCom," Deveraux said. "All right, ladies, deploy for attack. The clock is ticking."

"That's no ConCom," Taggart muttered. "Abort!"

"You're kidding," Maniac said.

"Baker Seven, you have no authority over this mission or its personnel," Deveraux barked. "You will obey my orders."

"Forget it. I've already analyzed those targets. They're Dorkir-class supply ships. They were deliberately left behind and out of harm's way. That ConCom is a Dorkir-class vessel as well—but it's not among them."

"You're saying they want us to attack those freighters, then they'll ambush us?"

"Not us, Commander. The *Tiger Claw*. She's at risk. We have to get back."

"You're a civilian scout. Why should I—"

"I hold the rank of commodore in Confederation Naval Intelligence, reporting directly to Admiral Tolwyn. My call sign is

Paladin. My security verification code is Charlie Six Alpha Zebra Niner. Try it, Commander. Now."

Blair couldn't wait for Deveraux. He plugged the numbers into his own computer's touchpad, attempting to tap into the Confederation Navy's Datanet. The left VDU blinked for a moment, then a message rolled across the screen:

> Commodore James Taggart
> Call Sign: Paladin
> Fourteenth Fleet
> Security Access Granted

"Holy . . ." Blair broke off in astonishment.

"Lucky guess," Deveraux told Taggart. "For all I know, you could've killed the real commodore and assumed his identity."

"Listen to me, Angel. That's all I ask. If I'm wrong, you'll have missed out on destroying a couple of freighters. If I'm right, the *Tiger Claw* could already be under attack."

"The *Claw* is already in the radiation belt, boss. They couldn't contact us if they wanted to," Forbes reminded her.

"Well, I ain't for turning tail," Hunter said. "I say we take out the freighters, *then* go back for the *Claw*."

"So we can pick through her rubble for survivors, Mr. Hunter?" Taggart asked.

"We're not taking a vote here," Blair said. "It's up to the commander. What do you say, ma'am?"

As Blair waited for her reply, he pictured the others doing the same. Forbes rubbed her eyes and wished she had spent more time sleeping. Polanski threw his head back and swore. Hunter unclipped his O_2 mask and stuffed an unlit cigar between his lips. Knight imagined with a shudder that a hundred fighters now buzzed over the *Claw*. Maniac itched with the desire to race forward and kick some Kilrathi butt. Taggart muttered a half-dozen "come ons" as precious seconds ticked by.

And Lieutenant Commander Jeanette Deveraux heaved a sigh and felt the absolute loneliness of her rank.

UNITED
CONFEDERATION
CARRIER *TIGER CLAW*

ULYSSES CORRIDOR

MARCH 17, 2654
0600 HOURS
ZULU TIME

7 HOURS FROM
CHARYBDIS QUASAR
JUMP POINT

"This is Black Lion Seven to Pride One. Getting a lot of interference from the belt. Scope's clear, but I don't trust it, roger."

On the *Tiger Claw*'s bridge, Captain Sansky shifted to the comm console, where Lieutenant Commander Obutu stood at Comm Officer Sasaki's shoulder. The screen showed the reporting pilot, Major Jennifer Leiby, her eyes narrowed, her face cast in the blue glow of display units. "Copy that, Seven," Obutu said into his headset. "Continue the sweep, manual as necessary."

"Aye-aye, sir. Think I see something now. Wait a minute. Is that . . . Bogies inbound. I say again—" A burst of static stole her words. "I'm hit! I'm hit! Mayday!"

Through the viewport and out past the Jovian-like planet's third moon, a speck of light burned brightly, then faded.

"Who's reporting in?" Gerald asked, bursting onto the bridge.

"Major Leiby," Obutu answered. "But we've lost contact."

Gerald's lip twitched. "What?"

"I read multiple targets inbound!" Radar Tech Harrison Falk said. The twenty-year-old stood before his tall, transparent screen and looked to Sansky, his face stricken.

Sansky regarded the viewport as Gerald and Obutu strained for their own view.

Dozens of small, glinting dots—and three larger ones—appeared from the cover of the third moon.

As Sansky turned back, Falk had already begun plotting the enemy's course. Obutu shouted commands to the security patrol pilots. The helmsman pulled up an evasion course on his screen. Then Gerald bolted to his command chair, dropped into it, and, after a nod from Sansky, shouted, "Battle stations! Battle stations! Launch all fighters!"

Sansky took one more look at the wave of enemy ships, then retreated to the captain's console, where he watched the attack as though it were a bad dream. The security patrol engaged the incoming fighters, converting the gas giant's ring system into a furball more deadly than any he had ever witnessed. Dralthi fighters double- and triple-teamed Confederation Rapiers, while the enemy's Krant medium fighters darted like wasps between ice and stone, vectoring toward the *Tiger Claw*. The viewports soon flooded with the images of individual dogfights, of fighters from both sides being run off-course to collide with asteroids. The carrier's eight dual laser turrets sent shudders throughout the ship as they fired upon swooping targets while throwing up clouds of shiny flak. Rapiers and Broadsword bombers arrowed away from the flight hangar to join the explosive fray, some torn to ribbons less than a kilometer from the ship and chain-detonating others.

Beyond the launching counterassault, on the fringe of the battle line, awaited the big Kilrathi capital ships. Pausing now so that their fighters could soften up the *Claw*, they would soon spring for the kill.

"All fighters launched, sir," Obutu announced, his voice sounding hollow and several lifetimes away.

Someone touched Sansky's shoulder. "Sir?"

Gerald's concern, an emotion he rarely displayed, brought Sansky back to the bridge, to the memory of his rank, his job. All was not lost—or gained—yet.

An automated voice rattled through the bridge's speakers: "Torpedo launch status: nominal."

"I count three dozen Kilrathi starfighters, two Ralari-class destroyers, and one dreadnought," Falk said, studying the holographic images on his display. "The cap ships are advancing at one hundred and twenty KPS. They'll be in firing range in four seconds."

Sansky glanced at Gerald. "Taggart was right."

"Maybe he knew something that we didn't. And if he did, then I'll brig him for withholding information."

"Worry about your bruised ego later, Mr. Gerald. Helm. Come about."

"Torpedoes incoming!" Falk cried.

A pair of Kilrathi torpedoes trailing thin plumes of exhaust followed a lazy curve, then shot headlong at the carrier.

"Launch countermeasures," Sansky said.

Falk nodded as the chaff clouds illuminated his screen. "Countermeasures away and . . . Torpedoes still on course, sir. Targeting port bow."

"Sound the collision alarm," Sansky ordered Gerald. "Rig the ship for impact."

The first missile exploded over the carrier's phase shields, tossing up lightning-laced rainbows of energy and debris that fell mercilessly upon her superstructure. Sansky clung to his chair as the second torpedo hit, and the bridge seemed to wheeze as the bomb choked it. Falk shouted something. Gerald grunted. Obutu demanded a damage report even as the blast wave persisted.

Sansky caught his breath and said, "Do we have a reply, Mr. Gerald?"

"We do, sir. Give me a target, Mr. Falk."

"Target acquisition imminent," Falk said, his voice cracking. "We have a lock!"

Gerald beat a fist on his palm. "Fire tubes one and two!"

Like unleashed bloodhounds, the two torpedoes sped away from the carrier, drawing chalk lines across the Jovian rings.

"Captain, I have visual from a Rapier near the destroyers," Comm Officer Sasaki said.

"On my screen."

The Rapier pilot spiraled through an incredible hailstorm of flak and laser fire, hurling himself toward an enemy destroyer, then pulling a six-G climb to break away. The image switched to his aft turret as two torpedoes slammed into the destroyer's weak shields and penetrated her hull armor. Twin shock waves ripped through ship's port side, dividing her amidships with underwater slowness. She spewed a huge, debris-laden gas bubble into the vacuum as hundreds of smaller explosions dotted her plastisteel innards. For a moment, Sansky thought he saw the Kilrathi themselves, giant bodies floating free and clawing for that green fog they breathed.

"Two direct hits, sir," Falk reported to cheers from the bridge crew.

The Rapier pilot kept broadcasting images, and Sansky grew calm as the dreadnought turned parallel with the remaining destroyer.

Her tubes opened.

A pair of torpedoes raced out.

There would be no stopping the Kilrathi now. *And a man*, Sansky thought, *must be true to his heart, especially at the end.* If he could manage that, then an apparent defeat would become a resounding victory. No one else would understand, but he would. And that was all that mattered.

Voices grew faint, muffled. Gerald shouted something about countermeasures. Falk's reply lacked hope. Then everyone screamed in unison as the enemy torpedoes struck a one-two punch across the phase shields.

Sansky rode the first shock wave, then fell to the deck as consoles crackled and smoked above him in a sudden moment of chaos.

"Comm is off-line!" Sasaki exclaimed. "Rerouting bridge to secondary."

"The phase shield is suffering a forty percent failure," Obutu added. "Battery room reports a fire. Torpedo room reporting damage. Unable to launch."

Sparks danced on Sansky's shoulders as he climbed back into his chair. Just outside the viewport, the remaining Rapiers struggled to lure the dozens of Dralthi and Krant fighters away from the *Tiger Claw*.

"I'm reading eight more targets from behind the dreadnought," Falk said.

Gerald made a lopsided grin. "They're sending in reinforcements."

"We should be flattered," Sansky said. He opened a comm channel. "Torpedo room. Report."

Spaceman 2nd Class Rodriguez, his eyes red from the smoke pouring into the station behind him, leaned toward the camera. "Tubes three and four damaged, sir. Autoloaders not operational. And we can't get back to one and two. The bulkhead's collapsed."

"Get me one tube back online, son. Can you do that?"

"I'll try, sir."

"We can't fire?" Gerald asked, springing to his feet. "Mr. Obutu. See if Mr. Raznick can spare some people to form a damage-control crew in Secondary Ordnance."

Obutu nodded and spoke quickly into his headset.

"Captain, scanning the cruiser," Falk said. "She's opening tubes."

"Of course she is," Sansky said calmly. "Of course she is." A shadow fell over him. He gazed into Gerald's worried face. "Commander?"

"The situation is dire, sir. If we're going to die, I suggest we ram them."

"We'll never get in that close."

"So we wait here to die?"

"Watch that tone, Mister."

"Captain. *Jay.* Let's go down fighting."

"I agree, sir," Obutu said, then looked to Gerald. "Damage-control crew on its way to the secondary ordnance room."

"Gentlemen. I have no intention of dying. Rolling over and playing dead . . . maybe."

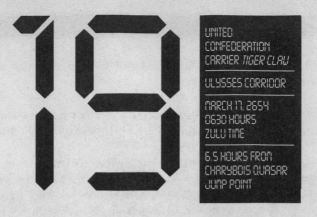

UNITED
CONFEDERATION
CARRIER *TIGER CLAW*

ULYSSES CORRIDOR

MARCH 17, 2654
0630 HOURS
ZULU TIME

6.5 HOURS FROM
CHARYBDIS QUASAR
JUMP POINT

"Mr. Obutu? Prepare to power down the entire ship," Gerald said, sliding back into his command chair.

"Power down the ship. Aye-aye, sir." A layer of sweat dappled Obutu's face, but his voice did not waver.

Sansky, noting the renewed hope in his crew, rose to pace the bridge. He did not share their faith in the plan, despite having suggested it. Powerless and adrift, the *Tiger Claw* would become an object of curiosity to the Kilrathi. The dreadnought's captain might bring his ship in close enough for the *Claw* to launch a sudden, point-blank torpedo—providing that Mr. Rodriguez and the DCC got a tube back online.

Or, as Sansky more likely figured, the big cat would note the power down, bare his fangs, and, without a second thought, blow the *Tiger Claw* into a memorial.

"Captain," Sasaki called excitedly. "I'm getting a friend or foe acknowledge from the new starfighters. They're ours, sir."

"It's Deveraux's strike force," Sansky said, guarding his emotions. The tide had still not turned.

But Gerald smiled back at the opportunity. "Mr. Obutu. Belay that power down. And find out how that DCC is doing in secondary ordnance."

"Aye, sir."

Flying in wedge formation, Deveraux's fighters, still just pinpricks of light, soared in behind the Kilrathi dreadnought and destroyer.

As a half-dozen targets presented themselves in Blair's HUD, instinct drove his gloved finger over the primary weapons trigger. He listened intently for the order to break and attack.

Deveraux hadn't said much since giving in to Taggart's pleas. They had returned to the *Claw* at full throttle, and when Forbes had sighted the destroyer and dreadnought, an odd mixture of relief, regret, and anticipation had filtered into the voices of Blair's comrades. Taggart had been right, but being right meant that the *Tiger Claw* had already faced a more powerful force without some of her best fighter pilots. Although Blair and company would now join the party, the *Claw* hardly stood a chance.

"All right, ladies. All Rapiers except Maniac and Blair engage those Dralthi."

Blair bit back a curse. "Commander, I didn't come out here as an observer."

"Relax, Lieutenant. Drama equals danger plus desire, and it's about to become dramatic."

"See you later, nugget," Forbes told Maniac.

"Watch yourself, Rosie."

The rest of the strike force peeled off in pairs to confront the Dralthi fighters streaking in at the wing's one o'clock low. Spiraling missiles and criss-crossing laser bolts produced a dense, expanding web that promised to snag any pilot who broke rhythm or got cocky.

"Broadswords, follow me in," Deveraux said.

"Roger that," Taggart responded. "Beginning the bomb run."

"Maniac? Blair?" she called. "Cover us."

Wrenching her Rapier into a forty-five-degree turn, Deveraux raced under and ahead of the Broadswords. The bombers throttled up and swept in behind her. She rolled to level off, spearheading the quintet.

"And here comes the flak barrage," Deveraux said.

The capital ships' big turrets spat and coughed up Triple-A fire that hung like handfuls of cotton balls tossed in zero G. And worse, the dreadnought's torpedo tubes opened to fire a salvo at the *Tiger Claw*, whose deck shields already cushioned rounds from dozens of strafing Dralthis.

Maniac's face popped up on Blair's left VDU. "Hey, man. Look!"

A mere kilometer stood between the *Tiger Claw* and the four Kilrathi torpedoes.

From his position, Blair could do no more than watch.

The torpedoes hit, and Sansky's command console tore apart. A jagged section flew up at him before he could block it. His head snapped back as the bulky panel struck his forehead. His face, once sticky with sweat, now felt warm and slippery. He lay back on his chair, his neck growing numb, his breath ragged.

Behind him, Obutu's voice penetrated the booming of lower-Deck explosions. "The hull has been breached at level three. Steering loss: eighty percent. Drone repair crew activated. Estimated recovery time: six minutes."

"Sir?" Gerald asked, standing somewhere nearby. "Sir? Medic! Medic to the bridge!"

"Blair? How's our six?" Deveraux asked.

"Clear for the moment," he replied, not that his report really mattered. The radar display—a living, breathing thing—could change in a heartbeat.

The proof lay in front of him as four Salthi light fighters shaped like upside-down V's broke formation to intercept the bombers. Blair tracked their velocity at nearly one thousand KPS, their afterburners blazing. One Salthi didn't pose a huge threat to a Rapier. But like killer bees, if you faced enough of them, they would overcome you.

A Dumb-Fire missile flared below Deveraux's starboard wing, then went from zero to 850 KPS in three seconds—enough time for the Salthi pilot she had targeted to curse her and beg for Sivar's forgiveness.

As Deveraux's Salthi vanished in a short-lived explosion, the fighter nearest it scissored across Blair's field of view. He dove after the Salthi, fixed his cross-hairs on the green circle leading the fighter, and dished out a flurry of bolts from his rotating nose cannon. The first bolt struck the Salthi's shields, crooked fingers of energy scattering across a light blue hemisphere. More bolts stitched a pattern across the Salthi's cockpit, and the ship flipped into a barrel roll before bursting apart.

Cannon fire from the cap ships cut through Blair's path as he strained to regroup with the bombers. He jammed the stick forward, plunging in a sixty-degree dive to escape.

But the autotracking systems aboard the cap ships refused to abandon their prey. The thick, deadly bolts returned, raking space along his Rapier's port side.

"It's getting too hot," Deveraux said. "It's up to the bombers. Let's get back out there."

Blair pulled up, flying below the bombers, then banked hard on a new heading for Deveraux's six. He switched to his aft turret camera and watched the bombers zero in on the destroyer's starboard bow.

"Thanks for the escort," Taggart said, then addressed Knight, who flew in first. "Steady on course. Wait for them to drop shields and open tubes."

Triple-A and tachyon fire clogged the space around the bombers as their defense computers automatically released clouds of chaff and decoy missiles.

"They're throwing up too much flak!" Knight screamed. His Broadsword's starboard wing grazed the expanding edge of a Triple-A cloud. Rivets popped as the wingtip tore off, violently rocking the bomber. "I'm hit!"

"Almost there," Taggart said, trying to calm the man. "Steady now. Steady."

Tachyon fire chewed into Knight's Broadsword, tearing open its belly to expose wires and pipes. Knight released a strangled cry as the bomber, now engulfed in flames, shattered across the destroyer's bow.

Taggart veered away from the flickering aftermath and vanished from Blair's screen.

"Maniac? You got visual of Taggart?"

"Negative. I think he booked."

"And that dreadnought's opening her tubes," Deveraux said.

Indeed, the huge vessel's tubes dilated open, and Blair beat a fist on his canopy. "Their shields are going down. We could've had them now."

The dreadnought's bow, shaped like two pairs of clamps forming a cross, raised as she passed over the first destroyer's wreckage. From one hundred meters below, the destroyer's tattered hull still glimmered, conduits jutting out like jagged teeth through lingering gas.

And from within that gas and those teeth, a ship appeared, a Broadsword, maneuvering thrusters firing to turn it up toward the dreadnought. "Baker leader. Get your fighters clear of the pulse wave," Taggart said.

"Roger that. Maniac? Blair? Break contact. Return to ship," Deveraux ordered.

James "Paladin" Taggart lifted a shaky hand to fire the Broadsword's two piggyback torpedoes. Then he touched another button, releasing the other two bombs from their belly racks. HUD reports indicated that all four of the mighty rockets had targeted the unshielded dreadnought.

Holding his breath, he lit the afterburners and climbed away from the cap ship. His gaze locked on the scrolling numbers showing his distance from the dreadnought. He shook his head. He was still too close. Then a proximity alarm beeped. He looked up to spot the Jovian planet's third moon, its heavily cratered surface lowering into view.

The torpedoes struck the dreadnought.

A nanosecond later, the entire Area of Operations stood under a tent of intense white light for one, two, three seconds . . .

The light dimmed to unveil a huge explosion tearing through the dreadnought, its hull shuddering as the widening rings of the blast wave stretched into space.

Caught unaware, the Kilrathi aboard the destroyer attempted to maneuver their vessel away from the wave, but the ship tacked only a few degrees before the blast wave hit. The destroyer tipped on its side, then collided with the first destroyer's hull, producing fires amidships that began cooking off its ammunition. An internal blast erupted through its hull, breaking off the bow in a fountain of sparks and jetting gas.

Taggart's grin didn't last long as he tracked the blast wave coming up behind him. It swallowed his exhaust, seemed to gain momentum, then struck his engines.

Displays crackled, fried, and went dead as the Broadsword groaned and took its beating. The bomber rolled, driving Taggart's head into the console. He felt the sting of a gash, and blood trickled into his eye. Blinking, he saw that the ship now barreled uncontrollably toward the moon. He seized the manual eject lever and jerked it down.

After a double click and faint blast of air, the cockpit ejection pod shot free, slowly rotating away from the doomed bomber, pushed to the edge of the weakening shock wave by sputtering retros.

The Broadsword impacted with the moon's surface in a cloud of ancient dust that would take days to settle.

Before Taggart could regain full control of the pod, he found himself caught in the third moon's gravitational pull. Rocking to and fro, he increased retros and tried to pull up from the cratered uplands. The retros teased him for a moment, then whooped and fell silent. He threw a toggle several times, trying to reactivate them. "Well, it was fun while it lasted."

As the gray and white surface hurtled toward him, he told himself that he had lived a glorious life, that he had inspired a young heart or two. James Taggart had accomplished what he had set out to do. He had lived the warrior's life and would die the warrior's death.

Nothing could be more fitting.

He grinned, remembering a few lines from his school days: "My mind misgives some consequence, yet hanging in the stars, shall bitterly begin his fearful date with this night's revels . . ."

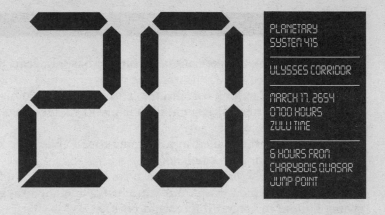

PLANETARY
SYSTEM 415

ULYSSES CORRIDOR

MARCH 17, 2654
0700 HOURS
ZULU TIME

6 HOURS FROM
CHARYBDIS QUASAR
JUMP POINT

Something jerked Taggart's ejection pod. He realized that he no longer plunged toward the moon. A Rapier descended beside the pod, and Taggart read the pilot's name along the cockpit's edge: Lt. Christopher Blair. The young man held his hand in a salute, which Taggart returned.

"You're bleeding, sir," Blair said.

Taggart touched the gash in his forehead. "And you had an order to retreat."

"Which I obeyed."

"Then why are you here?"

"Uh, I got lost, sir. Came looking for directions."

"Mr. Blair. Pilgrims never get lost."

Maniac's smile faded as the remaining Kilrathi fighters regrouped and began retreating behind the planet's moons. "Hey, Rosie? You want some more?"

The VDU flickered, and she appeared, lifting her brow. "Like you have to ask?"

They gunned their Rapiers in a sudden U-turn, chasing after the Krant, Salthi, and Dralthi fighters still in the open.

"Baker One to all Baker pilots. Return to base. Repeat. Return to base."

Maniac fired a look of disgust at Lieutenant Commander Deveraux before her image went dark in his VDU. He eased on his throttle and held course.

"Maniac?" Forbes called in a warning tone. "We just received an order to—" She never finished.

Two Dralthi fighters that had been trailing the pack pulled up and away from their wing. Like mechanized manta rays, they swung around to target Maniac and Forbes.

"They'll try to ram," Forbes said, one Dralthi rushing straight for her. She opened up with everything she had, tearing the fighter into scraps of superheated plastisteel.

The second Dralthi aimed for Maniac, and the enemy pilot's disgusting mug suddenly spoiled Maniac's display. If that weren't enough, the computer translated its taunt. "You will bleed for Sivar, you ignorant descendant of monkeys!"

Maniac let out a snort, then switched to Forbes's channel. "Watch this, Rosie."

Putting the pedal to the metal, Maniac howled as the afterburners threw him back. He centered his targeting reticle over the Dralthi—but he had no intention of firing. A collision alarm blared as the game of chicken continued.

"Shoot him, Maniac!" Forbes hollered. "Open fire!"

Realizing that the Kilrathi pilot had no intention of changing course and every intention of dying, Maniac rolled the Rapier to starboard. He express-delivered a volley of laser fire that sewed its way across the fighter's cockpit, mortally wounding the cat inside.

With only centimeters between them, the two fighters passed, the Dralthi now trailing nutrient gas and tumbling toward—

"Rosie!" Maniac cried. "Pull up!"

The Dralthi's wings acted like the blades of a fan to tear spark-lit gashes in her fighter's starboard side and belly. Forbes jerked the Rapier in an attempt to pull away, but the impact forced her into a roll. She throttled up to recover, flying straight but bobbing on invisible waves. One of her thrusters had been sheared away, and escaping fluids streaked her fuselage.

Maniac descended to form on her wing. "Looks bad. Eject and I'll tractor you in."

"My ejection system is fried."

He took in a deep breath. "Just stay with me, Rosie. We'll land together."

Ten minutes later, they neared the carrier's scorched flight deck.

"Baker Three and Four to Flight Control," Maniac said. "We're coming in for a side-by-sider. Clear away everything that ain't bolted down."

Boss Raznick, his beefy face hanging tiredly, replied, "Roger that, Baker Three and Four. Clear to land, SBS."

He and Forbes now flew level with the flight deck, bound for the energy field and the flight hangar beyond. He tossed a look to Forbes. Bad idea. The sight of her bobbing Rapier turned his blood icy. He checked their speed and approach vector. "We're coming in too hot."

"Sorry, but my brakes are in the shop."

"Line it up," he said, unable to smile, his gaze riveted on her fighter. "That's it."

"Piece of cake. Just like before."

"Except that you're right-side up." Now he managed a fleeting grin.

"I knew something was wrong."

Through his HUD viewer, Maniac watched the deck rush toward them. "Almost there."

Her wingtip tapped a wall next to the deck, but she wrestled the fighter straight as tiny groans escaped her lips.

"Okay. Easy. Just ease it in," he said. "Thirty meters."

"I got it." She could barely speak through her exertion. Her fighter lost power and fell behind his.

"Ten meters," he said as his own landing skids lowered and he glided over the flight deck, the energy curtain widening to fill his display. "Just five . . ." he trailed off as he realized her approach had gone awry. "Pull up! Pull up!"

But she didn't. She couldn't. Her port wing got caught on the flight deck's lip, and she started to flip over as the wing tore off and boomeranged away. The Rapier struck the deck with a gut-wrenching thunderclap, crushing her canopy. Shards of plexi floated away as the fighter scraped along the runway, then spun out to a halt, snapping off the remaining engine that rolled ahead of it.

Maniac frantically guided his Rapier through the energy field, then released his canopy before even landing. He climbed onto the Rapier's wing, then leaped off, bolting toward the hangar entrance, toward Rosie.

Someone familiar shouted his name. Shouted again. Loud footsteps. Then someone collided with him, arms wrapping around his chest, forcing him to the deck. He fell forward, bracing his fall, not bothering to look up at his assailant, his gaze consumed by the wreckage just behind the force field.

"She's outside the airlock!" Blair screamed. "You go through the force field and you're Jell-O!"

Maniac sprang to his feet. "Get me a suit! Get me a suit!" He started for the field as Blair seized his collar, holding him just a meter away. With the energy curtain so close that he could hear its hum, Maniac shivered as he realized that were it not for Blair, his panic would've driven him through it. He winced, staring at the twisted Rapier, then hollered, "Rosie! Rosie!" He could see her helmet, partially blocked by the shattered canopy. She did not move.

Fifteen minutes later, after Rosie and her fighter had been plowed off the deck and into space, Maniac stood facing a cold and angry Deveraux. Hunter, Polanski, and Blair gathered around.

"Lieutenant Marshall," she began. And she could stop there. Maniac knew where this was going. "You disobeyed a direct order to return to base."

"I was—"

"Which, during wartime, is considered treason and punishable by death. Hunter? Give me your sidearm."

Hunter exchanged a worried glance with Polanski as he withdrew his pistol.

Blair took a step toward them. "Hunter, put the gun away."

"She's the CO, nugget."

After a nod, Blair lunged toward Hunter, but Polanski intervened, driving his shoulder into Blair's chest. Much larger than Blair, Polanski had little trouble sliding behind his opponent. He locked Blair's arms to his sides.

Deveraux accepted the gun and raised it to Maniac's head.

Part of Maniac wanted to shout "Do it!" but another part believed she would.

"What's with you?" Blair cried. "It was a stupid accident. He has to live with it."

She looked to Blair, then at Maniac. "If you endanger another pilot, I *will* kill you." She handed the gun to Hunter, then strode away.

Polanski and Hunter turned their heated stares on Maniac.

He ignored them and jogged off.

21

UNITED
CONFEDERATION
CARRIER *TIGER CLAW*

ULYSSES CORRIDOR

MARCH 17, 2654
0800 HOURS
ZULU TIME

5 HOURS FROM
CHARYBDIS QUASAR
JUMP POINT

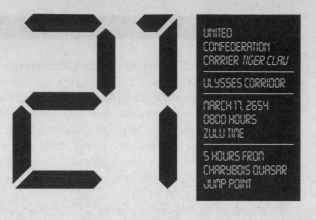

Captain Sansky had sustained a serious head injury. And worse, on his way to sickbay, he had suffered a heart attack. Commander Gerald now assumed command of the *Tiger Claw*. No stranger to the job, Gerald threw himself into the challenge. Without Sansky's interference, he felt certain he could save the carrier from another battle, one that would surely finish her.

During the attack, Sansky had seemed strangely unsure of himself. The Jay Sansky Gerald knew would have led them headfirst into the fight while barking orders and inspiring his officers to new heights.

But the old man had shut down, and Gerald refused to believe that fear had caused that. No, something else troubled the captain, and the captain's preoccupation left Gerald uneasy.

As he focused on the images coming in from the *Claw*'s tactical scanners and displayed on the helmsman's console, he cleared his mind of everything but the task at hand: finding cover from the Kilrathi battle group headed toward them.

Pictures from the Jovian-like planet's second moon revealed a string of deep craters, one of them large enough to conceal the carrier. "There," Gerald said, pointing at the screen. "Put her down there."

Once the carrier had glided over the crater, the helmsman lowered her into the shadows of the north wall.

"I think it's time for that power-down, Mr. Obutu," Gerald said.

"No problem, sir. Most of our systems are down anyway."

Gerald spared a smile over that irony. "Is the decoy ready?"

"Yes, sir."

"Very well. Launch the decoy."

"Launch the decoy. Aye-aye, sir."

After a barely perceptible thump, the decoy blasted away from the carrier. Gerald tracked its progress on a monitor. Long antennae extended from its circular hull, while a pair of dishes began rotating. The drone slowed a moment to compute its bearings, then fired thrusters and aimed for the Jovian-like planet's ring system.

Gerald turned his head at the approach of Taggart and Deveraux. He noted a hint of surprise in their expressions as the bridge lights faded, then winked out.

"Decoy away, Commander," Obutu reported. "Systems nominal. She has a bigger electronic signature than the *Concordia*. I think she'll fool them, sir."

"I hope you're right. Secure all active scanners. Passive systems only." He dropped into the captain's chair and looked up at a bank of scanners above the forward viewport.

The first moon hung in the right corner of one display, and as Gerald studied it, he noticed tiny shifts in its glow. Then part of that glow seemed to burn off and form into brilliant dots. One after another the moon shed those dots, and they spread into a triangular formation.

"There," Obutu said. "The Kilrathi battle group."

"They've missed us," Mr. Falk reported anxiously from his radar screen. He smiled broadly. "They're following the decoy."

The crew cheered. Even Gerald mouthed a "Yes!"

"Quiet!" Taggart shouted, startling everyone back into silence.

From that silence rose a steady beeping from one of Falk's passive radar detectors.

"I know that signature," Taggart said, charging toward the radar station. "It's a destroyer . . . hunting for us."

As if on cue, the beeping increased in pitch and rhythm. Falk's eyes bugged out. "They've spotted us!"

"No," Taggart said, his gaze shifting from the radar screen to the bank of scanners behind it. "We're still close enough to the radiation belt. Gamma rays are clouding their screens. If they don't see us, they won't find us."

Gerald found cold comfort in Taggart's assurance as the beeping grew more insistent. Out of habit, he swung his chair toward Mr. Falk, about to demand the destroyer's position.

However, with scanners down they were blind. He swung the chair back, then the deck lifted sharply.

"Did you feel that?" Deveraux asked, shifting to his side.

His chair shook as another vibration passed under the ship. He gritted his teeth and puffed air. "They're nuking every crater."

With that, the Kilrathi released another bomb whose shock wave rumbled through the carrier like a thousand ancient cavalrymen.

22

UNITED
CONFEDERATION
CARRIER *TIGER CLAW*

ULYSSES CORRIDOR

MARCH 17, 2654
0900 HOURS
ZULU TIME

4 HOURS FROM
CHARYBDIS QUASAR
JUMP POINT

The Kilrathi bombed many of the craters around the *Tiger Claw*. The bombing lasted for nearly an hour, and the ship was heavily damaged.

"The destroyer has moved on, sir," Mr. Falk said, observing its progress on his radar screen.

Gerald sighed and rubbed his tired eyes. "Mr. Obutu? Give me the numbers."

"Reports are still incomplete, but some of those bombs came very close. Thirty-five confirmed dead. One hundred and twenty-three wounded. We're still venting atmosphere on decks eleven and twenty-one. The breeches in Engineering and Secondary Ordnance have been contained. The flight boss reports hangar doors inoperative. No estimate yet on repair time. And he's still tallying up the damage to our fighters and bombers. It doesn't look good, sir."

"No, it doesn't. You have the con." Gerald pushed himself up and headed off the bridge.

As he turned into the corridor, Mr. Obutu's report rang in his ears. *How did it come to this?*

And his answer kept falling upon the arrival of three individuals.

He found his way to the lift and took it down to the living quarters. The rest of his journey became a blur until he reached Sansky's hatch.

Inside, he found the captain propped up in bed and connected to a half-dozen tubes and wires coming from a small rolling tower of sensors. The doctors had successfully cleared the blockage in his heart, yet they could not understand why his condition had not improved. "He says he wants to live," one doctor had said. "But somehow I don't believe him."

Gerald stood over the captain, whose eyes had trouble focusing. "How are you, sir?"

"They say the man is the ship, the ship the man."

"That bad, huh?"

Sansky managed a small grin. "Tell me."

After giving the captain a capsule summary of the *Claw*'s present condition, Gerald folded his arms over his chest and waited for a reaction. And to his astonishment, Sansky looked relieved. "Mr. Gerald, we could have sustained even greater losses were it not for your leadership. Thank you. I'm resuming command."

"Aye-aye, sir. But if I may speak frankly, we wouldn't have sustained any losses if—"

"I know where you're going, Paul. Stow that argument."

"Sir, they know our every move before we make it. And all since Commodore Taggart or Paladin or whoever he is came aboard with that half-breed and his reckless buddy. Then there's the question of the ULF signals. We didn't send them, yet Blair detected them. He's trying to throw us off his trail. In any event, it is my firm belief that there is a traitor aboard the *Tiger Claw*."

Sansky opened his mouth, but a ring came from the hatch bell. "Enter."

Taggart straightened and ran his finger along the sliding door. "This hatch is wearing a little thin, Mr. Gerald. Sound tends to carry right through it. So make your point."

"The boy's a Pilgrim. Could my point be any more clear?"

Grinning crookedly, Taggart crossed to the bed. "So he's a Pilgrim. In your eyes that makes him guilty of treason?"

"Yes, sir. It does."

"Barring the lieutenant's blood, do you have any other evidence that suggests he's a traitor?"

"We don't need any more evidence, sir."

"Lieutenant Blair risked his life to save mine today. He's as good as they get. And I've fought with the best. He can fly my wing any mission, any time. Now I urge you to get over that war, Commander. We have another to fight."

"Commodore," Gerald spat. "With all due respect to your apparent rank, you're a Naval Intelligence officer. You don't know anything about space combat, strategy, or war."

"I knew enough not to send Deveraux's wing on a wild-goose chase while the *Tiger Claw* was attacked."

"And if we had been destroyed, you would've been safely out of harm's way. Tell me, sir, was it just intuition that you knew about the Kilrathi diversion? Or are you withholding information?"

"Gentlemen," Sansky interjected. "None of this matters now. What matters is our survival and our mission."

"Both of which are threatened by this man's presence," Gerald said.

Sansky glared back. "Enough!" He proffered his hand to Taggart. "Welcome aboard, Commodore. Do you have any orders for me?"

Tensing, Gerald could not watch his captain shake hands with the half-breed's champion, a handshake that might seal their fate.

"Sir, this is your ship," Taggart said. "I offer you every assistance in the current crisis."

Gerald nodded. "Assist us by leaving."

"As matters stand, we need all the help we can get," Sansky said, lifting his voice, then lapsing into a cough. "This ship has suffered massive damage, and we have almost no operational fighters left. If you have any suggestions—any at all—I'd be glad to entertain them."

Taggart paced before the bed, eyes narrowed in thought. "The Kilrathi will be at the jump point in just under four hours, and we still don't know their capabilities or plan of attack." His hand brushed along the bulkhead. "I think this old lady's got a little fight left. All she needs is a little coaxing."

The man's foolishness surprised Gerald. "Engineering took a direct hit. Our fuel cells are nearly gone. We don't have enough power to keep up with the air recyclers, let alone get under way. Barring a miracle, we've failed."

"Failure is not an option, Commander," Taggart said. "And if it's a miracle we need, I suggest we find a way to make one. Understood?"

"Yes, sir."

"You're dismissed, Commander."

Wanting to choke the man instead of saluting him, Gerald went through the motions, spun on his heel, and left.

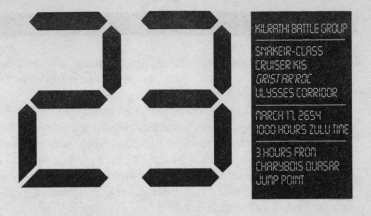

KILRATHI BATTLE GROUP

SNAKEIR-CLASS
CRUISER KIS
GRISTAR'ROC
ULYSSES CORRIDOR

MARCH 17, 2654
1000 HOURS ZULU TIME

3 HOURS FROM
CHARYBDIS QUASAR
JUMP POINT

23

Commander Ke'Soick looked toward the lift doors at the back of the bridge. Thiraka moved cautiously away from his captain's station, eyes trained on Admiral Bokoth. The kalralahr stood at the forward viewport, staring at the quasar.

"Kal Shintahr," Ke'Soick whispered, standing near the doors so that the admiral could not hear him. "I want to kill Bokoth. Permit me the honor."

"No."

Ke'Soick's lips curled back. "Then his trust in the Pilgrim will kill us all."

"Easy, my friend. It won't come to that."

"You've let it come this far, haven't you? He's of your clan. You have much more to lose. I understand, Thiraka. So permit me the honor."

"I won't sacrifice you."

"There's no other way. We must be aggressive, decisive, and above all, ruthless. *You* should lead this battle group."

"But I won't lead it without you."

"Kal Shintahr?"

Thiraka glanced across the bridge. The admiral had turned

from the viewport, his one eye panning the room. "Here, Kalralahr," Thiraka said. He hastened away from Ke'Soick and tensed as he arrived at the admiral's side.

"The whispering of young warriors troubles me," Bokoth said, resuming his study of the quasar. "As we grow older, our power shifts from muscle to mind. Does that shift weaken us? Hardly. But you don't believe that. You'd like to be rid of this old one who has taken over your ship and your battle group. Am I correct?"

Thiraka hesitated. "If I answer yes, I admit to treason. If I answer no, I call you a liar."

"And if you don't answer honestly, you will die where you stand."

Retreating a step, Thiraka said, "Your presence here weakens my authority. It reminds my crew that my own father doesn't trust me. And the loss of three ships—"

"I alone accept responsibility for those losses."

"You should have sent a larger force," came a tinny voice from the shadows. The Pilgrim approached them. "The *Tiger Claw* is alive and still a threat."

Bokoth flared at the traitor. "Go to the ConCom. Prepare the jump coordinates and transmit them to the fleet."

The human held his scowl a moment, then stormed off.

"What about the *Tiger Claw*?" Thiraka asked.

"We'll place the ConCom within range to find her." The admiral glanced at Thiraka. "You don't agree?"

"You serve the Emperor, Kalralahr. And I serve you." Thiraka bowed before his superior.

"That is no answer."

"For the moment, it is the only one I have."

After the bombing had stopped and the *Tiger Claw* had grown quiet, Maniac had fallen into a deep sleep, his body jerking as though the day's painful events were replaying in his subconscious.

Blair could have used some sleep himself, but he had too much on his mind. He returned to the flight deck, where he found pilots heading up their own maintenance teams. Three techs had already cleared the rubble from his Rapier. Although Blair's fighter had not sustained major damage, many of the other fighters and bombers, nearly one hundred in all, had fared far worse. Wings had been crushed, cockpits shattered, landing gear snapped off. Blair stared sadly across the great sea of mangled metal.

After catching the attention of his crew chief, he started toward the woman. Then he shifted course as he spied Deveraux. She squatted near her fighter's portside landing skid and stared up into the runner's compartment.

"Angel?"

She emerged from under her fighter, eyes swollen, hair disheveled. "What is it, Lieutenant?"

"Can we stop this game, please? I'm sorry about Forbes."

"Who?"

"Don't." He shook his head. "When a friend dies, it hurts. It's supposed to."

"You're the authority?"

"You can't forget the people you loved. They deserve more than that."

She closed her eyes. "What do you want?"

"Maybe I can help. Maybe we can help each other."

"I'm all out." She turned away.

"Maniac was crazy about her."

"He was crazy about her?" She spun to face him, all woman, all fire. "She was my best friend. I loved her."

"You weren't alone. You know he blames himself for what happened."

"And so he should."

"His confidence is shot. He's questioning every move he made. He can't go back up in that condition. And right now, we need every pilot we have."

"That's right. But you expect me to put him back on the duty roster?"

"Just do the right thing."

"I'll think about it."

"Maybe you can talk to the others. Maniac's a good guy. And he's sorry, really sorry. There's no reason for anyone to hate him."

◆   ◆   ◆

Twenty minutes later, Deveraux was summoned to the bridge. When she arrived, she saw Taggart at the radar station, staring into nothingness as the telltale beep of an incoming ship grew louder.

She headed for the transparent wall of the radar screen. "What's out there? Another destroyer?"

"It doesn't matter," Gerald called after her. "We can't take another round of bombardment."

Her expression grew hard, meant for him and Taggart. "I have four Rapiers ready to go. We'll go down kicking and screaming."

"We'll do better than that, Angel," Taggart said. "That ship up there is going to save us."

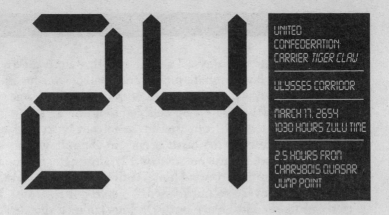

24

UNITED
CONFEDERATION
CARRIER *TIGER CLAW*

ULYSSES CORRIDOR

MARCH 17, 2654
1030 HOURS ZULU TIME

2.5 HOURS FROM
CHARYBDIS QUASAR
JUMP POINT

Maniac had tried to sleep, but Rosie's death played itself out in his dreams like a holo trapped in a loop. His chest felt heavy, and the thought of food made him sick. He had risen from bed and had accessed the ship's Datanet to lose himself in video recorded during the attack. But he found it difficult to concentrate and twice thought he sensed Rosie staring over his shoulder.

In short, living hurt.

Now he rolled onto his stomach. His pillow smelled like her perfume, and he took a deep breath, his eyes rimmed by tears.

Then he suddenly felt angry for what had happened. *It wasn't my fault! Do you think I wanted to get her killed?*

He wasn't sure who he had asked. God, maybe. The lack of a reply drove him farther inward, where he found his guilt waiting for him. He had not known Rosie Forbes for very long, but war affected time as efficiently as a gravity well. Two days or twenty years . . . it didn't matter. Life grew more intense when you lived on the border of death. You met someone, and in your minds you got married, had kids, retired, and died—all in the span of a one- or two-day stand-down. So Maniac had shared a lifetime with

Rosie during their two days. Then he had thrown it all away by believing that he had ultimate power and control over his life. The safe world, the just world, had died with her. He no longer trusted anyone or anything. And he believed in nothing.

An alert call echoed from the intercom, but it seemed distant and unreal. He buried his head deeper in the pillow and stared across a black void until he saw two Dralthi detach themselves from their wing and fly toward him. He fired all guns and launched all missiles, but every round missed. To starboard, Rosie's bright eyes flashed a second before both Dralthi slammed into her fighter. He jerked up from the pillow, his body rocked by chills.

"Lieutenant? C'mon. Open the door. Lieutenant?"

Someone had been calling him. "Come," he said, and the hatch slid aside.

Deveraux wore a new flight suit and had a computer slate tucked under her arm. "Let's go. Time to suit up."

He pulled the blanket over his boxers. "Ma'am?"

"I need my best pilots out there."

"I don't know if I'm one of your best pilots."

Her face drew up in mild disgust. "Does everyone here think I go around making *suggestions?*"

"No, ma'am."

"Then I guess I gave you an order. Be on the flight deck in five minutes." She turned to the hatch. "And do it for Rosie."

Deveraux left him floored. She had returned him to the duty roster, but more importantly, she had admitted the existence of a dead pilot. And that made Maniac suddenly want to live. To fight. He sprang from his bed, snatched up his flight suit, and fumbled with the zipper. Now it seemed okay to smile through his tears.

From a position just inside the *Diligent*'s loading hatch, Blair watched Commander Paul Gerald lead a squad of Marines up the ramp. Dressed in gray and red armored space suits and packing toy chests of anti-cat weaponry, the cocky jarheads appeared to have just blasted their way out of Hell's prison. Scarred faces and hardened expressions testified that they had made the escape more than once.

The commander also wore armor, and his presence had Blair frowning. During the briefing, there had been no mention of his going on the mission. "What is *he* doing here?"

"Let's find out," Taggart said.

As he reached the hatchway, Gerald gave them a dirty look.

Returning the same look, Taggart said, "I think you're on the wrong ship, Commander."

Gerald lifted a gloved index finger and aimed it at Taggart's nose. "I still have a responsibility to this crew, Commodore. And excuse my bluntness, but if you think I'm going to let *my* men be flown into combat by a rogue and a half-breed, you're sadly mistaken." He pushed past them.

Taggart winked at Blair. "He's really a great guy once you get to know him."

Blair grinned, then followed Taggart to the bridge. He saluted Deveraux as she noticed him.

"*Diligent*? You're cleared to launch," Boss Raznick said through the comm.

Taggart sat at the helm and looked to his console. "Roger, control. External moorings and power detached. Internals powering."

Gerald took a seat in the co-pilot's chair, looking as thrilled as ever.

The commodore guided the merchantman past the now-open and repaired hangar doors. The ship rocked a little as it parted the energy curtain and skimmed over the dark runway. They flew away through the crater's deep shadows and toward a trio of colossal asteroids. Taggart brought the ship behind one and rotated ninety degrees to port. The *Diligent*'s lines now formed with the asteroid's ragged ridge line, and the two Rapiers that ran escort hovered just below. Only a careful-eyed Kilrathi could spot them now.

"Passive radar engaged," Gerald said, his announcement punctuated by a faint beeping.

Taggart looked up, eyes distant as he interpreted the sound. "We have the target."

"There she is," Blair said, pointing to the forward viewports. A large ship glided overhead, her thrusters filling the bridge with a bright orange glow.

"That's no destroyer," Deveraux said.

Blair nodded. "It's the ConCom ship we came up against."

"They'll spot our heat corona soon," Gerald said.

"They won't have the chance," Taggart corrected. "Blair. Man the Ion gun." He opened a channel to the Rapiers. "Marshall? Polanski? Hit it."

Blair hurried off the bridge and through a long corridor. He found a ladder and climbed up into the gunner's domed nest, then buckled into his seat. The system activated, and he booted a pedal, swiveling 360 degrees in one fluid rotation. He took hold of the firing grips and got a feel for the Ion cannon's range of motion, its barrel extending about three meters from the transparent hemisphere. The asteroids and stars began wheeling around him as the merchantman broke from cover.

The ConCom ship veered away as the Rapiers chased after it and the escorts. Maniac performed a corkscrewing dive through a sleet storm of fire, juked right, then hit one of the Dralthis with a rapid fire of bolts that tore the fighter into sizzling sections.

"Yeah," Maniac shouted.

Polanski's Rapier overshot the second Dralthi, and his swearing crackled over the comm. The Dralthi tore after him, and Polanski led the enemy pilot on a tortuous, laser-lit course through the rubble.

With reflexes hotwired to the battle, Maniac pulled into an eighty-degree climb, aiming for the Dralthi on Polanski's tail. He fired upon the enemy ship and blew it out of the fight.

Then he spun to discover a pair of Dralthis rising from behind the moon. "Two more bogies at six o'clock." He squinted and opened up on one of the fighters. The Dralthi swerved out of Blair's glowing bolts and fired shots of its own that thundered across the *Diligent*'s shields. Blair cursed his unfamiliarity with the weapon. He should've had that fighter.

The ship jolted suddenly as Taggart increased throttle, bringing them up toward the larger ConCom ship. "Marines, to your stations," he ordered. "As soon as you get in, go straight for the bridge. We have to get control of that ship before they scuttle her."

Another Dralthi zoomed across Blair's sights. He pivoted to track the fighter and, grating his teeth, unloosed a barrage. The agile little ship darted to port, but Blair found it once more, this time locking on. An intense multicolored flash ended the cat's mission. "Yes!"

Now alongside the ConCom, the *Diligent*'s docking umbilical began to extend. Blair watched it for a second, then swung around, searching for more enemy fighters.

From a twelve o'clock bird's-eye view, Maniac looked down on a Dralthi as it made a kamikaze run for the *Diligent*. A long-range image from his forward camera showed the pilot wearing a dark helmet, the ship's bow reflected across its face. *Too bad*, Maniac thought. He wanted to see the terror in the cat's eyes as he parted the starry heavens like Sivar himself.

Turbines wailed as Maniac bore down on the Dralthi in his own kamikaze run. The pilot's head snapped back as the barrel-shaped nose of Maniac's Rapier sheared off the enemy fighter's cockpit. Maniac pulled four Gs to recover from the dive. He shot a look over his shoulder as the Dralthi did a pilotless dance and crashed into the ConCom's stern.

Damage reports flashed in Maniac's displays. The Rapier handled sluggishly, but Maniac didn't care. "That's for you, Rosie."

He arced back toward the *Diligent*. The ship's umbilical now latched onto the ConCom. A few seconds later, the Kilrathi ship's hull turned pink as the umbilical's lasers cut through.

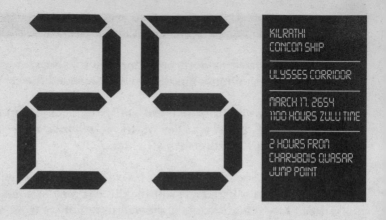

25

KILRATHI
CONCOM SHIP

ULYSSES CORRIDOR

MARCH 17, 2654
1100 HOURS ZULU TIME

2 HOURS FROM
CHARYBDIS QUASAR
JUMP POINT

Deveraux knew that the Marines did not like her leading them into the ConCom ship. But Deveraux's special schooling in enemy ship design made her the best person for the job.

Now she stood at the end of the umbilical, waiting for the hatch to blow open.

"Five seconds," a Marine reported, waving a small scanner near the cutting line.

Deveraux began a mental countdown, but the copper-colored section of plastisteel thudded to the deck before she reached one. She felt the umbilical's air tug on her shoulders as it fled into the Kilrathi ship. As suspected, the cats had turned off the artificial gravity in this section in order to slow the Marines' progress. She glided forward and turned into a triangular corridor clogged with a thick green gas and lined with conduits. A silhouette stirred ahead. She strained to see through the fog.

A yellow bolt tore a jagged hole in the bulkhead just a half-meter away. She returned fire, but she couldn't pick out a target. She touched a button on her helmet, engaging her thermal scanner. Data bars beamed at the corners of her faceplate. Forms grew more defined, details less so. The torn-up bulkhead glowed red.

The Marines charged in around her, cutting loose an incredible wave of laser bolts that stirred the alien gas into hundreds of tiny whirlpools.

"Hold your fire," she ordered, then studied the corridor. No movement or heat sources. "Tito! Marx! Take point. Second team. Watch our backs. Let's move."

Blair kept Polanski and Maniac in his sights as the two engaged another pair of Dralthis that had sprung from behind the asteroids.

"Lieutenant, can I have a word with you?" Merlin asked, his voice coming abruptly from the intercom.

"Little busy right now."

The hologram flashed into view and sat cross-legged on the Ion cannon's console. "I'm picking up some strange electromagnetic emissions from the Kilrathi ship. They're Pilgrim. The ULF frequency I picked up earlier."

"Can you pinpoint the signal?"

"Deck two, aft section. The bridge."

Decision time. Blair glanced at the radar display: all clear. Maniac and Polanski had destroyed the two fighters and could handle themselves for at least a little while. *Man, that's probably not true, but it makes me feel a little less guilty.* He lifted out his cross, kissed it, then climbed down from the gunner's dome. Moving quietly away from the ladder, he stole a glance at the bridge. Taggart and Gerald sat at their consoles, their backs to him. Good. He unlatched a rifle from its bulkhead mount, checked the charge, then fetched his helmet from the rack.

As he stepped into the umbilical, dense fog rolled toward him. Once he reached the opening to the ConCom ship, he could barely see anything. He turned into a corridor—

And something brushed his shoulder. He jumped back with a cry, lifting the rifle, finger tensing over the trigger.

A horrible thing floated next to him, a uniformed beast so ugly that nature had not yet forgiven herself for its creation. The thing's pale, long head had been torn open by laser fire, and its huge paws were locked in a death clutch. The corpse rolled over, and the yellow eyes twitched and stared at Blair.

Taggart had been right. The Kilrathi would not be entering beauty pageants any time soon. And Blair felt fortunate that his first close encounter was with a dead one.

"Nice," Merlin said through the comm. "I believe there's another way. To the right."

Blair started off and finally reached a door at the corridor's end. He frowned at the control panel labeled in Kilrathi.

"Translating," Merlin said. "Hit the big button."

"Of course."

Green fumes poured through the doors as they slid apart. He touched a control on his helmet, bringing the thermal scanner on line. He moved inside.

"Oh, no," Deveraux moaned as a half-dozen Kilrathi troopers ran up the corridor. The Marines traded a dozen bolts with the aliens, then fell back into an intersecting passage.

A sweaty and scared-looking grunt rounded the corner, ducking from incoming fire. "Ma'am? Got another squad moving in behind us. We are pinned down."

"Lieutenant Polanski? Report," Gerald ordered.

The young man's masked face showed on the comm screen. "No contacts, sir."

"I concur," Marshall added. "We're jamming local transmissions, but that doesn't mean our buddies didn't get off a signal. Better set the table anyway."

"Understood," Gerald said. "How 'bout you, Blair?"

No response.

"Lieutenant Blair? Answer your station." Gerald tapped on the ship's security cameras. "Look at this," he shouted at Taggart, pointing at the empty gunner's nest. "His orders were to remain on this ship." Gerald bolted up. "I'll find him."

Picturing himself with a gun shoved into Blair's forehead, Gerald slapped on his helmet and tore a rifle from the rack. He glanced to Taggart. *That's right, Commodore. You should look worried. Now your boy is going down.*

◆   ◆   ◆

"See that hatch up ahead?" Merlin asked. "That's the bridge. ULF signals are peaking the meter now."

After a second glance at the hatch, Blair dodged to the bulkhead. Large, cross-shaped windows built into the doors revealed two Kilrathi officers, their heads lowered to their consoles, their bodies outlined in the faint red of his thermal scanner. He cocked his rifle. Full charge. Keeping to the shadows and thicker fog near the wall, Blair stole his way to the windows.

On the other side, he saw that a third alien stood at a monitor while a fourth, probably the captain, turned to kneel before a copper-colored statue of Sivar. The captain's mouth moved.

"This is not good," Merlin said. "That Kilrathi in there just spoke a ritual phrase. He says that he's honored to die for the glory of Kilrah, the Emperor, and the Empire."

The captain rose and turned back to a center console, where Blair spotted a red button that needed no translation.

He fell back from the door, dropped an explosive round into his rifle's grenade launcher, aimed, and—

With a faint thump the bomb left his weapon, struck the door, and blew it off its tracks in a column of flames edged in black smoke. Blair rushed toward the hatch, then crouched to pick a target.

The Kilrathi captain jerked away from the red button as Blair's first round struck its shoulder. Two more bolts punched the now-howling captain to the deck, beside an officer who had been killed in the explosion.

Blair flinched as the remaining two bridge officers returned fire from the cover of consoles. He dodged through showers of sparks and flying debris, then dropped to his stomach behind a long row of stations. From between the widely spaced console legs he saw armored feet closing in on him from flanking positions.

One, two, three!

Blair rolled under the stations and popped up behind a warrior, jabbed his rifle into the thing's long head, and fired. The alien collapsed.

But where was the other officer?

Pivoting frantically, Blair couldn't find him.

"Nicely done," Merlin said, seated on the forward edge of a nearby monitor. "The last Kilrathi has fled."

"Thanks for the help."

"I'm just running my program. And by the way, don't touch the red button."

He looked at the self-destruct switch. Then he saw a black box on the station he had hidden behind. Many cables ran from the box, some leading to a monitor that scrolled numbers and letters, some into a bank of consoles he guessed were part of the ConCom's communication system. He set down his rifle and lifted away a piece of plastisteel from the door he had shattered. His mind raced as he read the words PEGASUS NAVCOM AI. "They have the Charybdis jump coordinates, Merlin."

"They have more than that. The *Tiger Claw* is using a special code to broadcast its location to the enemy. The only people who have access to that code are Captain Sansky and Commander Gerald."

"So one of them is a traitor!"

"Lieutenant, someone is—"

Reacting to the sound of footfalls, Blair whirled to lock gazes with Commander Gerald. The big man raised his rifle and started into the bridge. "You'd like my ship to fall, wouldn't you, you treacherous piece of garbage." He gestured with his weapon toward one of the dead Kilrathi. "I should feed you to these things."

"Looks like you'll get your chance," Blair said, then patted the Navcom. "They owe you a few favors, don't they, Mr. Gerald?"

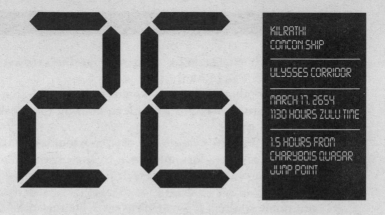

KILRATHI
CONCOM SHIP

ULYSSES CORRIDOR

MARCH 17, 2654
1130 HOURS ZULU TIME

1.5 HOURS FROM
CHARYBDIS QUASAR
JUMP POINT

Gerald crossed the ConCom's bridge in several long, deliberate strides. "Mr. Blair," he began, then suddenly smashed Blair's helmet with the butt of his rifle. "I believe you just called me a traitor."

Blair rolled across a console, then fell to his knees.

After flipping the weapon around, Gerald aimed it at Blair's head. He pulled the slide back, then nodded at the NAV-COM. "Turn it off."

Three simple words . . . yet they shocked Blair. If Gerald wasn't the traitor, then—

A hollow laugh resounded from the rear corner of the bridge. "To think we came from you."

Wearing a space suit and holding a large Kilrathi pistol, a man stepped from the shadows, a man whose thin face seemed familiar, but Blair couldn't think of a name.

"Wilson?" Gerald said, his tone so full of surprise that the word had barely escaped his lips. "But the Pegasus—"

The admiral took a step forward, and Blair had never seen a man more consumed by hatred. "Twenty years of service. Ironic, isn't it?" He extended his arm, the pistol directed at Gerald.

"Wait," Blair cried. He lifted his cross with a trembling hand.

Wilson drew back, gazing suspiciously at the cross, then at Blair. "Where did you get that?"

"It was my mother's. She was killed at Peron." Extending a palm in truce, Blair slowly got to his feet, holding the cross like a shield in front of him.

For a second, Wilson's eyes glazed over, as though he had taken himself across the light-years and back to the massacre. "When you remember Peron, what do you feel?"

"I feel hate."

"So you think you're a Pilgrim? Prove it." He raised his chin to Gerald. "Kill him."

Blair's nod came easily, and he turned back for his rifle. He had enough bitterness stored inside to fight Gerald, but could he kill the man? The answer was obvious.

"No rifles," Wilson said. "Use the blade."

Shifting back, Blair pulled the cross from its chain and touched the center symbol. The cutting edge flashed out.

Gerald withdrew a long, ugly-looking fighting knife from his vest. "I was right all along. Come on, Pilgrim. Pass your test." The commander lunged at him.

Blair backed up and slipped behind a console. He climbed on top of the station and leapt into an open area, near the helm controls. Gerald followed. Now they circled each other, jabbing with their blades.

Suddenly the commander whirled around, boot raised, and kicked Blair in the ribs. As Blair fought to remain standing, he saw Gerald lift his blade—

A horrible tearing sound came from the sleeve of Blair's space suit. He reached for the tear. Automatic voice alarms warned him that Gerald's blade had penetrated the suit's first layer.

He tensed once more as a wild-eyed Gerald searched for an opening. The man's blade shot at Blair once, twice, a third time, and Blair blocked each assault.

Then he grabbed Gerald's wrist with his free hand. He threw himself beneath the commander and swept out the man's legs. Gerald landed hard on his back as Blair rolled over and centered his blade over the man's heart.

"Finish him!" Wilson cried.

He looked at Gerald, whose face grew colorless in the half-light. The commander mouthed a curse, and Blair felt as though he had been dipped in ice water. He imagined Gerald screaming in agony. He lifted the blade a few inches, preparing to drive it home—

Then turned, flicking his wrist.

The blade swished through the air, threw off flashes of gold and silver, then . . .

Thump!

The admiral flinched and looked down at the cross stuck in his chest. His space suit began hissing loudly. He stumbled, reaching blindly for support, then slumped against a column.

Gerald sat up and went to the admiral, whose face looked white and bony. "Wilson!"

Despite his agony, the man remained awake.

"Why warn Tolwyn?" Gerald demanded. "Your Kilrathi friends could've destroyed Pegasus, taken the NAVCOM, and jumped to Earth with no interference."

He smiled weakly. "I'm a Pilgrim. And the stars were the Pilgrims' destiny. Not Earth's. Not Kilrah's."

A faint click drew Blair's gaze to the admiral's hand. Wilson had just triggered a concussion grenade!

"C'mon!" Blair cried, already turning to retreat. He crashed into a pair of big chairs as he and Gerald darted toward the hatch.

At the first hint of the explosion, they dove toward the corridor. An intense wave of heat wiped over Blair's legs as he hit the rattling deck. His comm unit crackled as the boom overloaded his mike. He crawled toward the corridor, but a second explosion had him cowering again. Black smoke poured over them, and the snapping of flames grew louder. He forced himself to stand and took a deep breath. Gerald was already on his feet.

"Now do you want to know who your traitor is?" Blair asked.

The hatch at the corridor's end opened, drawing Gerald's attention. A Marine crouched near the edge, directing the business end of his rifle at the commander. "Halt!" he shouted as two other Marines joined him.

"Deveraux?" Gerald called back.

Deveraux jogged from behind the Marines and through the hatch. "Sir? What are you doing here?"

"Never mind. Secure the fuel cells. Blair and I have some business to take care of."

Blair and Gerald returned to the *Tiger Claw*, fetched pistols, then rushed into Captain Sansky's quarters like military police.

The captain sat up in bed, his sickly face showing only mild surprise. "Gentlemen, I don't pose a threat." He checked his watch. "In fact, I'll be dead in a few minutes." Noting Blair's frown, Sansky waved a finger at a needle lying on his nightstand. "In the old days they used cyanide. The plecadome, I'm told, makes for a more peaceful retreat."

"Jay. You were the best CO I had." Gerald lowered his pistol and huffed his disappointment. "Why?"

"Because, Paul, sometimes the role you play isn't the one you were born for."

"You've failed at both," Gerald growled.

"Have I?" he asked, his voice heavy with irony. "A bad spy and a bad captain." His eyelids grew heavy as the poison took effect. He battled against it, lifting his hand toward Blair. "Here. Give this back to Tolwyn. Please."

Blair took the ring as the admiral's hand fell limp. He held the ring tightly, needing something to believe in for the moment, something tangible, something that wasn't a lie.

"Commander?" Obutu said over the intercom.

"Talk to me, Mr. Obutu."

"Engineering reports that the Kilrathi fuel cells have arrived. They'll have them adapted in a few minutes. They estimate that we'll have sixty percent power."

"Very well. Prepare to get underway." Gerald shook his head at Captain Sansky. "I can't believe what he did . . ."

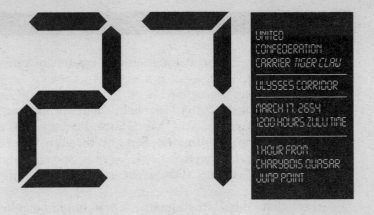

27

UNITED
CONFEDERATION
CARRIER *TIGER CLAW*

ULYSSES CORRIDOR

MARCH 17, 2654
1200 HOURS ZULU TIME

1 HOUR FROM
CHARYBDIS QUASAR
JUMP POINT

Blair felt a distinct jolt as he stepped onto the bridge. The *Tiger Claw* floated up, and the shadows folded back to expose the pockmarked and grooved surface of the crater's wall.

Lieutenant Commander Obutu lay on his back, assisting a tech with repairs on the portside observation station. The other officers stared determinedly at their screens, making reports into headsets.

"I heard about Sansky," Deveraux said, meeting Blair at the rail. "Gerald's not going to inform the crew until we're dead or out of this. He's breaking regs, but he's right. We have to keep morale high, speaking of which, how's yours?"

"I'm all right."

"Wow. Very convincing."

"I'll be all right. Soon. Maybe."

"At least now you're honest."

He gestured toward Taggart, who stood behind Gerald's command chair. "I need to speak with him." Deveraux released him with a nod, and he crossed to stand at attention beside Taggart. "Sir, I have something for you." He fished out Tolwyn's ring.

Taggart grinned at the sight, then shook his head as Blair

offered it to him. "Keep it for now. We get out of this, you can return it yourself."

"Thank you, sir."

"We're clear of the crater," the helmsman abruptly reported.

"Very well," Gerald said. "Mr. Obutu. Prepare a drone. Input the Kilrathi jump coordinates. Send it through the Charybdis Quasar to Admiral Tolwyn."

"Aye-aye, sir." Obutu slid out from beneath the observation station.

Gerald glanced back to Taggart. "They should be able to target the exact location of the Kilrathi jump entry. It'll be over before they can get their weapons on line."

"If Tolwyn's there, Mr. Gerald. If he's there."

"Sir, we have a problem," Obutu said. "All communications and decoy drones are off-line. Executive override."

"Sansky," Gerald said as though swearing. "Without those coordinates, Tolwyn doesn't have a chance—and we're too big to slip past the Kilrathi and warn the fleet."

Taggart gave Blair an appraising glance, then said, "We'll have to send a fighter through."

"Impossible," Gerald argued. "There are over a thousand singularities in that quasar. To jump it would be suicide without Navcom coordinates."

"We don't need a Navcom, Mr. Gerald." Taggart placed a hand on Blair's shoulder. "Lieutenant, you will navigate the quasar. Lieutenant Commander Deveraux will follow your lead."

Stunned by the order, Blair's voice cracked. "It's statistically impossible, sir."

The commodore tightened his grip. "We don't have another option." His voice lowered to a near whisper. "You have the gift."

Blair slid out of Taggart's hold and looked to the deck, reaching for his cross—but it wasn't there. "I don't have the faith."

"It's not faith," Taggart said, coming up behind him. "It's genetics. It's the capacity to feel magnetic fields. But if you believe you need faith—" He circled in front, reached into his tunic, and withdrew a Pilgrim cross. "Here. Take mine." He tossed it to Blair.

Awestruck, Blair studied the cross, then gazed curiously at its owner. "Why didn't you tell me?"

Taggart cocked a brow. "You didn't ask."

The reverence in Taggart's eyes when he had examined Blair's cross and the pain he suffered when speaking of the Pilgrims were now clear.

"Long-range scanners are picking up Kilrathi ships, sir," Obutu told Gerald. "Looks like a destroyer and a cruiser."

"Mr. Blair. Can you do it?" Gerald asked.

"I think so, sir."

"Not good enough, Lieutenant!"

"Sir, I can do it, sir!"

"Very well. I'll have the Kilrathi jump coordinates transferred to your Rapier and copied to Deveraux's. We'll create the diversion. Just get those coordinates to Tolwyn."

"Aye-aye, sir."

On the flight deck, Deveraux hurried off toward her fighter. Blair continued along the flight line toward his own Rapier.

"Pilgrim," a familiar man called out.

Blair craned his head as Hunter came toward him. His muscles grew tighter with the pilot's every step.

"I heard what you did on that Kilrathi ship," the big Aussie said. "We all heard. I was wrong." He extended a hand.

Trying to hide his feeling of relief, Blair took the hand and gave the pilot his firmest shake.

"Good luck." Hunter ambled back to his Rapier.

As Blair turned, he found Maniac standing in his path. "You trying to sneak out and die without me knowing?"

"I—"

"Uh-uh, don't say anything. I want to remember your pretty face just like this. See you on the other side, bro." He banged fists with Blair, then winked and dashed off.

Blair continued on to his fighter, and once there, he settled into the cockpit as the commotion outside came to a roar.

Within sixty seconds the deckmaster waved him into position for launch. He saluted, got clearance from Raznick, and for the first time in his military career, he felt uneasy about punching his thrusters. The Rapier accelerated through the energy curtain and over the runway. He flipped on his VDU and watched the *Tiger Claw* shrink into the vast sea of darkness. Deveraux formed on his wing. She sent him the order to maintain radio silence as they approached the asteroid belt.

28

UNITED
CONFEDERATION
CARRIER *TIGER CLAW*

ULYSSES CORRIDOR

MARCH 17, 2654
1245 HOURS
ZULU TIME

15 MINUTES FROM
CHARYBDIS QUASAR
JUMP POINT

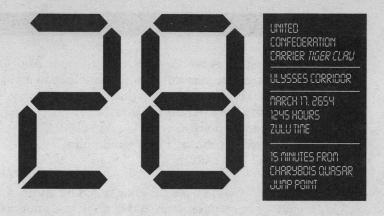

"Report!" Gerald yelled as an alarm sounded on the bridge.

"I have a bogie, vector one-nine-seven mark three," Mr. Obutu said, "approaching at a velocity of . . . now it's gone. Attempting to reestablish contact, sir."

Taggart studied Obutu's display, then breathed a curse. He moved to Mr. Falk's primary radar screen.

"You have something, Commodore?" Gerald asked.

"It's a Skipper missile. Must be a prototype. We only pick it up when it decloaks to take a radar fix."

"Can we stop it?"

The Commodore shook his head, then quickly snapped toward Mr. Falk. "Estimated time until impact?"

Falk plugged the coordinates into his terminal, then waited for the results on his big screen. "Nine minutes, sir."

Blair peered at his radar scope. The contact had disappeared. Time to break radio silence. "I had a strong signal at ten o'clock, headed toward the *Tiger Claw*. Now it's gone."

"Accessing intelligence database," Deveraux said. "Give me a sec. All right. Here we go. Contact is a Skipper missile."

"Can the *Claw* take it out?"

"The only thing that can kill it is a starfighter in visual contact." With that she banked hard right, breaking from his wing and climbing above the asteroid field.

"Hey, what are you doing?"

"Stay on course. Get through that jump point."

"Angel? Angel? Don't do this."

"ETA on missile?" Gerald asked, feeling his pulse surge.

"Six minutes, five seconds. It should decloak in a minute or so," Falk said.

Mr. Obutu spoke quietly into his headset, his expression holding little promise. "Sir, we can't take a direct hit."

Gerald nodded gravely, then found Taggart's empty gaze. "Commodore, isn't there anything we can do?"

The man slumped in his chair. "It's in Blair and Deveraux's hands now."

Blair jolted as the blip reappeared on his display. "It's back, Angel. Check your scope."

"I got jack," she said. "Come on . . . wait . . . got it!"

Deveraux's fighter, now a blue blip on his screen, chased after the red blip. "It's off to your starboard, bearing two-two-four by one-three-one."

She followed his coordinates, winding toward the contact.

"I'm coming back to assist."

"Negative."

He lit the burners and slammed the steering yoke right, riding the tube of an invisible breaker. Her thrusters gleamed ahead, and she fired lasers at the missile as it cloaked. She continued to lead the Skipper, directing her bolts along its course.

"Angel. You're too close," Blair said. "Back off."

A sudden and harrowing explosion erupted ahead of her Rapier. The Skipper shimmered into view and corkscrewed through space, casting off jagged hunks of red-hot plastisteel.

"Target destroyed," she reported tersely, then pulled up to escape the tumbling debris.

But her report had come too soon. The Skipper exploded with a burst like an antique flashbulb. The light gave way to a visible shock wave. Circles of force tore through space and swept up Deveraux's Rapier as though it were a paper airplane in a typhoon.

Her scream shocked Blair. "Angel! Angel!"

The Rapier's wings tore off as it rolled through the wave. A faint burst of light came from her canopy as she ejected. The escape pod rode the crest of the wave, then suddenly broke free as retros slowed its progress.

Blair held fast to the stick as the remnants of the explosion rocked his fighter. He turned ninety degrees and flew parallel to the wave, nearing the pod and the long line of wreckage floating beside it. The pod's retros fired again, rolling it upside-down relative to him. He flew under Deveraux, then slid up so that his cockpit stood within a meter of hers. "You okay?"

"Nothing broken," she said, staring down at him through the Plexi.

Blair regarded a panel at his elbow. He touched a button, bringing the system online. "Hang on. I'm going to tractor you back to the ship."

"No. Go on. We can't both disobey orders."

"I'm not leaving you here, Commander. You'll be out of air in an hour."

"An hour and four minutes."

"You're going back to the ship."

"You disobey my direct order, and I'll have you court-martialed."

"Like I care."

"Then care about the billions who will die if the fleet doesn't get those Kilrathi jump coordinates."

She had spoken the truth, a truth that broke his heart. "You're all right, Angel. Guess you know that."

She unclipped her mask and smiled, then pulled off her glove and placed her hand on the Plexi. "You, too, Chris."

He could barely look at her as he touched his thruster control, sliding away from the pod.

That soft face. That hand pressed on the glass. He would never forget her.

Gerald swiveled his command chair toward the radar station. "Repeat?"

Falk gazed at his screen in wonder. "I said there's no sign of the Skipper missile, sir. One of the Rapiers must've shot it down."

"Where are they now?" Taggart asked, staring thoughtfully through the viewport.

"One continuing on course, and one . . . picking up an auto beacon from an ejection pod." Falk jerked his head toward another quadrant on his display. "Got two Kilrathi ships at extreme range."

"Yes, that's about right," Taggart thought aloud. "Knowing our condition they would only send two, keeping the rest for an ambush at the jump point."

Rising, Gerald joined the commodore at the viewport. "So what now? We have just a half-dozen operational fighters and can barely maneuver."

The commodore faced him with a renewed zeal in his eyes. "What now, Mr. Gerald? Now we make the Kilrathi on those ships sorry they were ever born." He regarded the bridge crew and roared, "Battle stations!"

"Kilrathi cruiser and destroyer are in missile range," Falk said anxiously. "They're launching."

Taggart's eyes widened. "Open fire, Mr. Gerald."

"Aye-aye, sir." He switched on the shipwide comm. "All batteries, fire as she bears."

Deveraux had powered down all but the most vital systems in the ejection pod—especially its auto beacon that would give away her location. She shivered as the pod grew colder than a Belgium winter. Out to port, missiles streaked across the blackness, creating rainbows of vapor. She strained for a better look, but her breath condensed on the Plexi. She wiped it away and took a tiny, rationed breath.

◆   ◆   ◆

Blair reached the edge of the asteroid field, then flipped over his HUD viewer. *All right, all right,* he thought, trying to calm himself as he took in Charybdis's colorful fury. Her reds seemed like blood, her blues like veins. He maxed out the throttle and leaned over to power up the jump drive computer. A pair of screens showed multiple glide paths through the quasar, all of them wrong. Or at least they felt so. "Merlin? Check my coordinates."

The hologram directed his voice into the Rapier's comm. "Coordinates A-okay, boss. Three minutes to jump."

"Firing jump drive." He touched the switch—

And an enormous six-G jolt struck the Rapier as the drive drop-kicked him forward. His lips flapped, and his cheeks flirted with his ears.

The quasar smeared into a striped tunnel, and thousands of ghostly claws tugged at the fighter. The stick felt as though it were melting in his glove. As he got closer to the quasar, the jump drive made noises like a wounded animal.

"Ninety seconds to jump point," Merlin said. "But you're drifting off course."

"Negative. The quasar's gravity is affecting you."

"No, it isn't."

"Merlin . . ."

The little man wisely fell silent. Blair skimmed the jump drive screens, then shut his eyes.

Mother, you don't want me to come here. But I have no choice. I hope you'll understand. I hope you won't stop me.

"Warning. Jump drive system reaching point five light speed, PNR velocity for this system," the ship's computer said. "Do you wish to continue?"

"Affirmative."

"PNR velocity achieved. System lock activated. Pilot, you are committed to the jump."

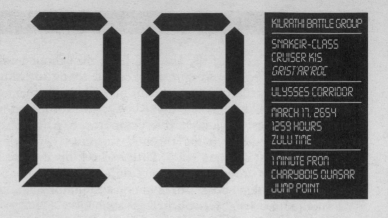

29

KILRATHI BATTLE GROUP

SNAKEIR-CLASS
CRUISER KIS
GRIST'AR'ROC

ULYSSES CORRIDOR

MARCH 17, 2654
1259 HOURS
ZULU TIME

1 MINUTE FROM
CHARYBDIS QUASAR
JUMP POINT

Admiral Bokoth's plans were falling apart. But Captain Thiraka would not wave his earlier doubts in the admiral's face. He felt more comfortable now. He had decided to let Ke'Soick kill the admiral. Thiraka would sacrifice the life of a dear friend for the preservation of the Empire. As agonizing as it was to lose Ke'Soick—who would be executed for the admiral's murder—Thiraka had come to see the truth and the honor in disposing of Bokoth. He bowed before the old one. "Kalralahr. A manned Confederation fighter is approaching the quasar with its jump drive engaged. We're not in position to intercept."

"A fighter?" Bokoth asked, turning in the command chair. "Using what coordinates?"

"Apparently the right ones, sir. The ship is on course."

Bokoth's good eye bulged. "He's going to warn the Confed fleet of our jump coordinates. Follow him. Instruct all ships to mark our course but follow original coordinates through. Sixty-second intervals."

"As you wish." Thiraka nodded and stepped away. He gave the new orders to the helm, then stood beside Ke'Soick.

"Now?" the commander asked.

"I agree with his orders," Thiraka said. "We'll wait until after the jump. But don't worry, my friend. You'll have your chance."

Gerald did a double-take as he watched the Kilrathi cruiser turn hard to port, away from the *Tiger Claw*. "Mr. Falk?"

"She's changing course, sir."

"Mr. Gerald," Taggart said. "Prepare to lower our shield. Starboard missile battery prepare to fire."

After setting the shield to perform a flash shutdown, Gerald discovered an error in Taggart's order. "Sir, the missile guidance systems won't activate at this range."

"They won't need to. Arm warheads."

So many vibrations rumbled through Blair's Rapier that he swore he now plunged into an atmosphere, a degree away from burning up.

"Merlin?" he shouted, warping the computer's name. "Velocity?"

"Light speed mach-point-eight-two," the little man responded, his voice as shaky as Blair's. "Twenty seconds to jump. Can you do it?"

"Only one way to find out."

When Blair had plotted the course through Scylla, he had closed his eyes, fingered the touchpad, and played a song of coordinates. He had obeyed the feeling and felt the need to surrender to it now. "Computer. Switch to voice recognition and prepare to plot course."

"Acknowledged. System ready."

He reached out with his mind, with his body, into the quasar, feeling his way through a transparent maze of gravity and magnetic fields. Then he pictured the correct coordinates and spoke the numbers.

"First set of coordinates plotted. Warning. Deviation in jump course found. Do you wish to adjust course?"

"Ignore deviation. Maintain speed and heading."

The *Tiger Claw* approached the Kilrathi cruiser head-on. The enemy ship fired thousands of laser bolts that weakened the

Claw's shields. Soon the two great ships would pass each other, headed in opposite directions.

Gerald buckled into his seat, seeking courage in his torpedo status display. "Commodore. Four tubes loaded and online. Warheads armed. Range of target: four hundred six meters and closing."

Taggart sat in the command chair, his face tight and serious. He clutched his armrests and leaned toward the Kilrathi cruiser as though he would leap at it himself. "Lower shields. Give 'em a broadside, Mr. Gerald."

"Fire all batteries!" Gerald cried.

"Aye-aye. Fire all batteries," came the reply from the starboard ordnance room.

Kilrathi cannon fire continued to hammer the now-unshielded cruiser in rumbling waves, but Gerald ignored it, focusing on the four torpedoes. Three shot through the cruiser's shield to impact on its hull, tearing up portside batteries and a launch bay. The fourth torpedo found the ship's bridge and blew it into a billion pieces.

As the cruiser tipped over, a dozen of the *Claw*'s guided missiles burrowed into her hull, stopped short somewhere inside the ship, then exploded. Fiery light filtered through the cracks and holes.

"Hey, Maniac? Where are you going? Don't leave my wing!" Polanski shouted.

Maniac continued in his eighty-degree dive to escape the raging dogfights over the cap ships. "Two Krants broke loose. They're after the *Claw*. If they hit the Ion engines, the ship'll be dead in space. Now don't leave my wing!"

"I'm with you, buddy."

The blue blip that was Polanski's Rapier slid onto Maniac's radar display. "Take the one going for the bridge. I'll get the other."

"He's really moving," Polanski said.

"Get him, man! Get him!"

Jamming the stick back, Maniac pulled out of his dive and streaked toward the carrier's stern. He targeted the Krant swoop-

ing down on the *Claw*, and his VDU showed that the pilot had
missile lock. Maniac hollered his war cry and issued last rites to
the cat with Neutron guns. Once a fighter, the Krant blew into a
flaming trail that blocked Maniac's path. "Whoa, whoa, whoa,"
he muttered, going upside-down. Showers of burning fuel
splashed on the Rapier's belly. He angled away, and the last of the
fuel burned off.

From his new position, Maniac saw that the *Tiger Claw* glided
alongside the cruiser at point-blank range. "And they say I'm
crazy."

A flash at his port quarter gained his attention. Polanski's
Rapier cut a jagged line across the heavens. "That's six kills today,
Maniac. You won't top me."

"Oh, no?" Maniac pinned the throttle and went straight up like
a missile. The enemy fighters rushed toward him.

"Hey, don't do anything reckless," Polanski warned. "Not
without me!"

The jump drive shrieked, and the rattle had become a single noise
that made it almost impossible to concentrate. "Second set of
coordinates at four-seven-five-five-three-nine-nine," Blair shouted.

"Warning. Course deviation. Do you wish to—"

"Stay on course."

"Five seconds," Merlin reported. "Four, three, two—"

The striped vortex winked out of existence.

"Mother?"

*You shouldn't do this to yourself, Christopher. You weren't
meant to see me. This is not your continuum.*

It is mine. I chose it.

You don't have the right to choose. Only one does.

*What do you mean? There aren't any rules. I feel this. I can do
what I feel.*

Then you'll fall. Like the others.

You're not my mother, are you?

*I'm everything your mother was, is, and will be. I'm in every
part of the universe at once, as you are now, as you shouldn't be.*

Why?

I wish you could understand. I wish that more than anything. But I've seen your path. And there's nothing I can do to change it.

Wait. We've had this conversation before. This has already happened.

No, it hasn't. But it will.

I don't understand.

You don't need to.

Where are you going? We have to talk! I need to know—

Thunder overpowered his words. Suddenly, the harness dug into his shoulders. His head fell forward, then ripped back. Star lines whirled, grew shorter, formed into points as the jump drive turned off. The faint smell of heated metal passed into his O_2 flow. He blinked to clear his vision, then squinted at the stars and knew, knew with his eyes and with his blood, that he was on the edge of the Sol system. "We did it," he muttered. "We did it!" He patted the canopy. "I love this baby. She held together."

"I'm not sure I did," Merlin moaned.

Blair quickly dialed up a secret Confederation channel on his comm system. "This is Lieutenant Christopher Blair of the TCS *Tiger Claw* calling any Confed ship. A Kilrathi battle group has the Charybdis jump coordinates. They'll breech at one-six-seven mark eight-eight-nine, Sol system. Do you read?"

Only static replied.

"Merlin. Check your frequencies for signs of the fleet."

"Nothing . . . Wait a minute. Check behind us."

"Behind us?"

The still and silent darkness exploded in a terrific white circle filled with webs of energy. A giant, ferocious-looking carrier flew out of the circle.

"Kilrathi capital ship," Merlin said. "Snakeir-class."

Blair pounded the instrument panel. "We're too late!"

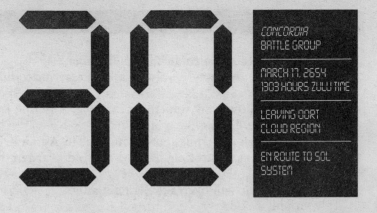

CONCORDIA
BATTLE GROUP

MARCH 17, 2654
1303 HOURS ZULU TIME

LEAVING OORT
CLOUD REGION

EN ROUTE TO SOL
SYSTEM

Admiral Geoffrey Tolwyn had pushed his battle group to one hundred and twenty percent, having lost a total of five ships on the way to Sol. But he had reduced the Kilrathis' two-hour lead down to a mere three minutes. No battle group in the history of the Confederation had made better time. Commodore Bellegarde had said they would have to break every jump record to reach Sol within forty-two hours. Tolwyn had embraced the challenge.

The *Concordia* would soon reach Pluto, then head for the bluish, ringed dot of Neptune.

"Are you all right, sir?"

Tolwyn did not look back at Bellegarde. "Have you come again to suggest I sleep, Commodore? Because—"

"No, sir. Comm reports a faint message from Lieutenant Christopher Blair. He's in the system and broadcasting the Kilrathi jump coordinates."

That sent Tolwyn spinning around. "Blair?" Was it a coincidence? Hardly. "Like father, like son."

"Should we respond, sir?"

"Identifying Confed Rapier," Radar Officer Abrams called out.

"He's heading toward Earth at LSM point nine."

"What is it, Mr. Abrams?" Tolwyn asked, reacting to the man's troubled voice.

"He's being followed by something massive, Admiral. I've analyzed its signature. Looks like a Snakeir."

Bellegarde tensed. "Permission to intercept it, Admiral?"

"No," Tolwyn said, stroking his two-day-old beard in thought. "We wait."

"But the Snakeir will overtake Blair's fighter."

Tolwyn only nodded.

"Sir, if we don't intercept, that ship will reach Earth orbit before us. The casualties could be significant."

"I'm bloody well aware of that, Richard." Tolwyn bolted from his chair and spoke through gritted teeth. "All ships are to hold their positions and target those jump coordinates."

"But . . ." Bellegarde trailed off. He thought a moment, then his mouth opened in realization. "Ah, if we jump him, we'd be out of position when the Kilrathi fleet comes through."

"We're after bigger game than that Snakeir. We need a resounding victory—or this war is over." Tolwyn faced the stars, their age-old light seeming to shine on his own past. "For that victory, I have to risk the lives of innocent civilians and one very brave young lieutenant."

Blair ran the diagnostic twice, and twice he cursed the damage to his engines. Yes, the Rapier had survived the jump, but now he could only pry eighty-seven percent thrust from the machine.

And the massive blip on his radar screen inched closer.

"Blair to Confed fleet," he said shakily. "Do you read me? Kilrathi capital ship has penetrated the quasar jump point and is in Earth space. Copy?"

Static upon static.

"Confed fleet, do you copy?" He threw back his head. "If they're here, they're out of range. Earth will never see the Kilrathi coming."

"Ironic that we made it this far," Merlin said. "Of course, irony is an essential ingredient in every tragedy."

"Shuddup. Or at least help us out."

"I knew this was all going to end horribly. Did I mention that we'll be in range of the Snakeir's guns in ten minutes?"

"At least they can't launch torpedoes at this speed."

"I'm sorry, Christopher. But they won't have to."

A radar alarm beeped rhythmically, and Blair stared through his HUD viewer. "There! Got a contact dead ahead. It's the fleet signaling. They've heard us!" He opened the channel. "Blair to Confed fleet. Kilrathi capital ship on my course, aft of my position. Confed fleet, do you read me?"

The alarm drummed louder. Blair checked his scope and saw the blip. "Only one ship. But it's huge."

"It isn't a ship," Merlin said in a dire tone. "Check your scanners."

Blair engaged the telescopic scanner, its readout now rippling across his HUD. Space shimmered for a moment, then cleared to show a lonely beacon signaling in the night. He glimpsed a data bar for identification.

And wished he hadn't.

Beacon 147.

"All we need," Merlin grumbled. "Scylla. Bane to sailors and monster of myth."

"Report on Lieutenant Blair?" Taggart asked Mr. Obutu.

"We're not sure, sir, but we think one of the Rapiers jumped."

Taggart turned to Mr. Falk, ever standing behind his large radar screen. "What about the locator beacon from that Rapier pod?"

"Nothing, sir. Lost contact during the battle."

"We've sacrificed too many good pilots already," Taggart said sadly. "Have the *Diligent* prepared for launch. I'm going after that pod."

"Aye-aye, sir."

The commodore double-timed off the bridge, growing more anxious as he imagined Deveraux or Blair slowly dying in that cramped durasteel box.

"Christopher? Why haven't you changed course?"

Blair sweated over the controls and had trouble listening to Merlin over the wail of the proximity alarm. He would shut it down, and a moment later it would return. "Merlin, can you turn this thing off?"

"I will, but in case the alarm hasn't cued you, you'll be past Scylla's Point of No Return in ninety seconds. Its gravitational pull will tear us to pieces. More precisely, to minute, highly dense particles."

"Solutions, Merlin! No more problems." Blair glimpsed the stars as they contorted into the gravity well's whirlpool of space-time.

Solutions. The word rang in his head and sparked an idea. Blair had a Snakeir behind him, a gravity well ahead. Solution? In his mind's eye he saw one, but it seemed crazy. Still, it was the only one he had. "How much does a Snakeir weigh?"

"Accessing specs. About two hundred thousand tons, give or take a few thousand."

A smile passed over his lips. One throw of a switch, and the afterburners slammed him into his seat. Space seemed to open up around him as he bulleted toward Scylla. Warning lights now dotted Blair's HUD, but at least Merlin had successfully turned off the proximity alarm.

"What are you doing?" the little man cried. "The afterburners will use all our fuel."

"I know, but I need more thrust. Eighty-seven percent won't cut it." Excitement tingled along his spine.

"But we're still headed for that thing!" Merlin cried.

Captain Thiraka took in a long breath of nutrient gas, then went to Bokoth, who sat in the command chair and looked for all the Empire like the vandalized statue of a war hero. "Kalralahr, planetary torpedoes online. We are almost in range. There is no response to the Rapier's transmissions. Sivar smiles on us. The surprise is total."

Bokoth's lips flared. "Yes," he said slowly, "it is."

Something punched into Thiraka's back, found a seam in his armor, and penetrated flesh. The sudden agony felt so severe that he shamed himself by screaming. Rigid in shock, he turned.

Commander Ke'Soick held a bloody *vorshooka* blade, the ritual instrument for cub bearing and murder. "Forgive me, Kal Shintahr."

"He's a skilled warrior," Bokoth rasped through a sinister grin.

"You won't die quickly, Thiraka. I wanted you to see our victory and know, really know . . . regret. How dare you plot my murder. Did you really believe that Ke'Soick's loyalty could not be turned?"

"My father will have your life," Thiraka said, collapsing to his knees.

"I kill you *with* your father's consent. The Kiranka clan will soon be clean."

Thiraka's shoulders grew numb, and he realized he could no longer lift his arms. His thoughts were swept into a storm of panic. He thought of calling for help, but who would listen? Who would dare defy Bokoth?

Second Fang Norsh'kal suddenly rang the ancient tocsin to alert the bridge crew.

"What is it?" Bokoth demanded.

Hissing nervously, Norsh'kal delivered his report. "The Rapier is homing in on a beacon signal. It could be a Confederation guidance buoy."

"Or a capital ship," Bokoth corrected, then winced as he forced his old body toward the infrared monitor in front of him. "Identify and report. Full battle stations."

On the admiral's screen, Thiraka saw a red speck heading toward the beacon.

And he suddenly realized where they were and what that beacon marked. He opened his mouth to warn Bokoth, then smiled. The Rapier pilot had become an ally in revenge.

Deveraux had thought she could die peacefully. She had thought she might experience a warm state of bliss before the cold draped her in an eternal sleep.

She had been idealistic about death.

Now reality had stolen most of her air. Reality had iced up her canopy so that even the pleasure she took from the stars was gone. *I did all right*, she thought. *It wasn't such a bad life. I helped some people. I wasn't as selfish as I could've been, I guess. If only I could take this cold. But I can't. I'm a fighter, but I can't take this. Call me weak. I don't care anymore.*

She reached for the pod's main panel, her hand shaking so

badly that she could barely bring her finger down on the correct button. The panel lit.

"Self-destruct system armed. T minus thirty seconds until self-destruct," the computer said. "System will lock out override at T minus five seconds."

Blair gazed at his HUD, never more determined. A half-dozen warnings kept lighting his screens. He blinked sweat out of his eyes and checked the rear turret display. "They're still back there," he told Merlin. "Good."

"If you say so. Kilrathi radar locked on. Ten seconds to the Point of No Return . . . and you're almost out of fuel. You won't be able to turn."

"Give me a count."

"Four . . . three . . . two . . ."

He jerked the stick hard to starboard, but the engines coughed before responding. Numbers clicked backward on his velocity gauge. Five and a half Gs pinned him to the seat. "We're not going to break free," he cried, eyeing another gauge. "We don't have enough fuel."

"You've got ten more seconds of thrust."

"Not enough!"

"Then find a weakness in the gravity field. Feel it."

Every rivet, plate, wire, and switch seemed to cry in protest as the Rapier grappled with Scylla. Blair projected himself into her swelling arms and felt for a way out.

He pulled the stick back, climbed a moment—

Then abruptly dove while slaloming away.

"Three seconds of thrust."

With a last jerk, the Rapier tore from Scylla's clutches, rocketing away at a ninety-degree angle.

"We're free," Blair said, only half-believing it.

Thiraka had lost the use of his legs. He poured all of his energy into breathing. He could no longer smile as he watched Bokoth foolishly chase after the Rapier.

Second Fang Norsh'kal shouted, "Kalralahr, the Rapier has veered away! Confederation ship, dead ahead."

Bokoth nodded and took a second glance at his screen. The horror that befell his face thrilled Thiraka. "That isn't a ship! Hard to port! Reverse all thrusters!"

Blair's engines sang a decrescendo and died. The Rapier glided through space. The silent cockpit felt eerie.

"We're out of fuel," Merlin said. "And battery power's nearly exhausted."

But Merlin's report seemed unimportant because a beautiful sight took form in the distance. The huge Kilrathi Cap ship sailed straight for Scylla's open mouth, its retros and reverse thrusters firing weakly against her mighty pull. "The Kilrathi's too heavy," Blair confirmed. "Scylla's got her."

Thiraka battled to lift his chin as the gravity well bloomed across the starboard viewport.

"All engines full!" the admiral shrieked, his face draining of color.

Norsh'kal jolted from his sparking console. "Engines overheating!"

Bokoth shrank to his chair. "But Sivar chose us." He looked down at Thiraka—

Who used his remaining strength to shake his head and stare angrily at the admiral.

Behind them, a bulkhead burst open. Nutrient gas rushed toward the gaping seam and jetted into space.

Ke'Soick and Norsh'kal screeched and pounded past Thiraka, their bodies stretching unnaturally toward the viewport and gravity well beyond.

Suddenly the world became dark, and the cries faded.

Thiraka wondered if he had died, then, through the numbness, he sensed his body being pulled apart.

"Record this, Merlin," Blair said, marveling at the Snakeir as it turned sharply to port in a final effort to dodge Scylla.

The well flung the ship around and drew it in, stern-first. Cracks opened across the Snakeir's hull, met other cracks, then released colossal sections that formed a parade of wreckage stretching toward the vortex.

Blair could not see Scylla's mythical six heads as they devoured the ship, but their effect humbled him. In less than ten seconds, the last pieces of the Snakeir's bow spun into the well, leaving a fleeting band of distortion behind them.

"Can I stop recording?" Merlin asked.

"Yeah."

"What's wrong? We got them."

"I know. I just can't imagine dying that way."

"Then how does freezing to death sound? You've got four minutes of battery power."

"Send an automatic distress, along with the jump coordinates."

"I already have. No ships in range."

"Then that's it. We're dead."

"Christopher, if you die, I cease to function. Your father made me that way."

Blair unclipped his mask and palmed sweat from his face. "I'm sorry."

"When people know they're going to die, they confess things to each other, say things they—"

"What is it?"

"You don't know much about how I was designed. Your father wanted it that way. But I don't believe he wanted you to die without knowing. My chips were made with protein from your father. It was his way of never saying good-bye."

"But he did leave."

"In the physical sense, yes. He knew he would. He loved you, Christopher. More than anything. And he wanted me to show you how much. I hope I didn't let you down."

"You didn't," Blair said with a half-grin. "How could you ever let me down?"

CONCORDIA
BATTLE GROUP

MARCH 17, 2654
1315 HOURS ZULU TIME

SOL SYSTEM
PERIMETER

KILRATHI JUMP POINT

Admiral Tolwyn held his breath as the *Concordia* decreased thrust and the battle group spread into attack formation.

"What do you think, sir?" Bellegarde asked as they stared ahead. "Are we too early or too late for the party?"

Tolwyn squinted at a flickering gleam in the distance, a gleam that quickly burst into a ring of light "We're right on time." He favored the radar officer. "Identify that ship."

"She's a Fralthi-class cruiser," Abrams said.

"Fire all batteries."

Laser bolts and guided missile exhausts knitted a hundred transparent trails into the gap between the Fralthi and the battle group. Tight-lipped, Tolwyn observed the bombardment and noted another ship flashing through the jump point.

Even as he faced Abrams, the young man shouted, "Ralari-class destroyer in our sights, sir."

"Take her out."

Pummeled by a surprise attack, the Fralthi got off only a half-dozen rounds, then produced a spectacular light show as it broke apart. The destroyer plowed into the Fralthi's wreckage, then took four torpedo strikes to her stern.

"They're coming through one ship at time," Bellegarde said. "They have no chance to defend themselves or warn the ships behind."

Tolwyn nodded. "But where's that Snakeir?"

"She's disappeared from our scanners."

"Launch two Rapier wings and a squadron of Broadswords. We have to find her."

"Aye-aye, sir."

The status light on Blair's life support panel faded. He probably had a couple, maybe three more minutes of oxygen left if the cold didn't kill him first. The shivering had come, grown worse, and now he sat with chattering teeth, rocking himself toward death.

His Rapier had glided well past Pluto. Far beyond the gas giants and beyond Mars lay that precious planet, homeworld of humans, the only home, some said. He wanted to go there and see the legendary beauty that everyone fought so hard to protect. Too late now.

"Hey, Merlin. You there?"

With the fighter's systems down, the little man took holographic form, his image flickering on Blair's knee. "Here, Christopher."

"You were right all along."

"I was?"

"We're doomed."

Merlin folded his arms over his chest and glared like a drill sergeant. "Don't say that. You're a fighter. So fight. We're going to make it."

"Cold got to you, Merlin? You sound downright optimistic."

"Let's just call it intuition—"

Blair fell forward as the Rapier lurched.

"—or a working array of scanners."

"What the . . ." A powerful spotlight shone on the cockpit. The light panned away, and behind it floated a Broadsword bomber that literally brought tears to Blair's eyes. The pilot snapped off a salute, and Blair managed a shaky reply.

◆   ◆   ◆

"TCS *Tiger Claw* entering low Earth orbit," Abrams said.

Tolwyn gasped as he surveyed the old carrier's shattered and blackened hull. When Gerald had made his report, he had obviously understated the ship's condition. As expected, the commander had spent more time discussing his disappointment and disbelief over Captain Sansky's actions. Tolwyn had taken the news with only moderate astonishment. Sansky wasn't the first or last traitor to wear a Confederation uniform.

The lift doors opened, and a familiar young man hurried onto the bridge, looking about as tattered and battle-weary as the admiral himself. Lieutenant Blair brightened as he met gazes with Tolwyn, then steered himself to the viewport.

Tolwyn returned the boy's salute, then proffered his hand. "Your father would've been proud."

"Thank you, sir. And it's an honor to finally meet you." He stood starry-eyed a moment, then jolted. "Oh, I almost forgot. I have something for you." He removed a ring from his breast pocket. "Captain Sansky asked me to return it."

Tolwyn took the ring, eyed it with a deep affection, then slipped it on. He tried to mask his sorrow over Sansky's betrayal, but Blair's reaction said he had failed. "The wounds of civil war run deep. He was a good captain, despite everything."

"Yes, sir. And sir? Did anyone locate Lieutenant Commander Deveraux?"

"Paladin went after her. No word yet."

Bellegarde, who had been sitting at an observation station, went to the comm console. He spoke to the officer there, then slipped on a headset. "We're monitoring the *Diligent*'s transmissions. She's been in contact with the *Tiger Claw*. Commodore Taggart's requesting clearance to land."

The young lieutenant hurried toward Bellegarde. "Is she with him?"

"Lieutenant Commander Deveraux is on board," Bellegarde said, concentrating on the signals.

"I knew she'd make it," Blair said with a hearty nod.

"Taggart is requesting an emergency medical team to meet him on the flight deck immediately."

Blair froze. "What's wrong?"

"I'm sorry." Bellegarde pursed his lips and removed his headset. "The rest of the transmission got cut off as they entered the *Tiger Claw*'s airlock."

The lieutenant's expression held more than simple worry over a comrade. Tolwyn smiled inwardly. "Mr. Blair? I think you're on the wrong ship."

"Sir, if I can borrow—"

"Get down to the flight deck. I'll have a fighter waiting for you."

He charged toward the exit, remembered his salute, then knifed through the lift doors before they had fully opened.

Blair switched off the comm in his borrowed Rapier, cutting off Boss Raznick's shouting. The boss would have to forgive Blair's reckless approach. He plowed through the energy curtain and blew the canopy as the Rapier came to a roaring hover and abruptly landed.

Standing in his cockpit, Blair spotted the *Diligent* across the hangar. A crowd had gathered near her loading ramp. He jumped from the fighter, then sprinted toward the commotion.

Taggart, Gerald, and Maniac stared over the shoulders of two medics as they struggled to revive Deveraux. She lay on a lowered gurney, and her back arched as one medic waved a pen-shaped device over her heart.

Maniac moved off from the group. "You made it!"

Blair couldn't take his eyes off Deveraux. "What about her?"

"Pure luck that I found her at all," Taggart said. "She must've turned off her beacon so as not to tip off the Kilrathi. She had eight seconds left on her self-destruct when I nudged the pod, woke her up, and got her to deactivate. She passed out before I got her moored. Brave girl."

He slipped past Taggart and dropped to his knees beside Deveraux. Her ashen face made him tremble. "Come on, Angel. Come back. Don't you die on me." He took her cold, limp hand in his own. "Come on, Angel."

Maniac stooped down next to him and placed a comforting hand on his shoulder.

The grim-faced medics continued waving their instruments over Deveraux. One placed a small disc at the base of her neck and studied readings on a palmtop scanner. "Hold on now. Wait. Yeah, there it is. I got a pulse."

"That's right, Angel," Blair said, squeezing her hand. "Don't you die on me."

Her eyelids fluttered and finally opened. She coughed a little, then turned her head and smiled through her grogginess. "What did you say?"

"I said don't you die on me."

She licked her parched lips. "Is that a suggestion or an order?"

"That's a definite order," he said with a stifled laugh.

Their gazes locked, and she did not look away. Her lips welcomed him. He learned toward her, going in for the kiss—

"We have to get her down to sickbay," one of the medics said, blocking Deveraux's face with his arm. He winked. "Don't worry. She'll be fine."

Blair stood as the medics raised the gurney and wheeled Deveraux toward the lift doors. He kept his eyes on her until she rounded a cargo container, out of sight.

"So, Mr. Blair," Gerald began. "I heard you single-handedly took out a Snakeir. Lured the ship into that gravity well at one-four-seven."

"That's correct, sir."

"Well, despite that, despite everything, I still don't like you." The commander flicked an ugly stare at Taggart's cross. "However, you've earned a little of my trust. In all likelihood, I'll be assuming command of the *Tiger Claw*, and I want only the best wing commanders I can find."

Taggart rolled his eyes. "The commander's trying to promote you, Lieutenant. I understand he's got a short list of command-approved wing commanders. You want the job or what?"

Blair grinned at the joke. "Wing commander? Me?"

"I can use you, Lieutenant," Gerald said. "We stopped the Kilrathi—"

"They'll be back," Taggart cut in. "The only question is when."

"We'll be ready for them this time," Blair said. "No more surprises."

"He'll take the job," Taggart told Gerald with a wink.

"I don't know," Maniac said, having been remarkably silent until now. "Maybe it's just me, but I didn't think they were all that tough."

Gerald and Taggart looked at Maniac as though he had finally lost his mind. Even Blair could not hold off his frown.

"What?" Maniac asked, feeling the heat. "I mean it."